La Segunda Guerra Civil Americana

-

THE SECOND AMERICAN CIVIL WAR

Book I

1

TABLE OF CONTENTS

Chapter 1

HOLIDAY

"We didn't feel listened to", a Patriot told me. That might have been the most honest thing I heard any of them say during the entire war, but by that point I'm not sure I was listening either. My name is Alba Rubio Diaz, a veteran of the European intervention into the Second American Civil War. I want to relate this story as I think only I can, given how close I was to some of its central events and participants. History is a story often told by the victors for their own reasons, but my only wish is to tell the story as it happened.

Life can be so very present during wartime, and that has a real attraction. Many soldiers will admit to the adrenaline rush. Some speak about serving something greater, but most will tell you that they serve for the soldiers next to them. I agree with all of that. Of course this is a story of events and great conflict, but ultimately of people, and the people I served with were truly heroes. I especially wanted to tell of my friend and fellow soldier, Hugo Garcia Lopez, a natural leader (and already an experienced operator) who brought us through many of our most violent days in America. He had an appreciation of life, and of music, that stayed with us.

Every effort has been made to compare dates and events with the available records and with other soldiers from that campaign to ensure a truthful version, though parts of it still seem unbelievable (even to me). I have changed names where necessary for national security, and made certain highly sensitive data more obscure to protect sources and methods.

Pride at having served in Spain's armed forces is one thing, but nostalgia and regret are two sides of the same coin. I would not trade the experience, sculpting myself with those years, but I also wish that things had gone differently. Most soldiers in the Special Forces of any nation, if they are honest, will admit that they *want* to be in the middle of it. Whatever it is. Wherever it is. If there is something big happening, they want to be sent in. They want to contribute, to serve. But, dear reader, the world is a delicate place, and easily broken. The stronger you are, the more gentle should be your hands. The sharper your mind, the less cutting should be your words. It is hard to reconcile how little moments of understanding hold the world together each day, and maintain it. These moments are sometimes the only thing preventing annihilation. It is noble for man to fight against evil but, without understanding, the horror will all be repeated in time.

Americans held the pale hope that a second civil war wouldn't happen, not to them, and yet it did. Spaniards, like everyone else, had followed the news of America's war with China, and afterwards when the next president was elected. We followed it on the news, when the turmoil and political division got steadily worse. We saw the unrest, the economic hardships, the rise of openly violent militias, the worsening storms, the breakdown in society, the refugees, and finally the chaos that was the second American Civil War. In the following months I learned first hand how little I really knew about the situation. I served in Spain's special forces with the Fuerza de Guerra Naval Especial (FGNE), one of few women to do so at that time. This, of course, put me in a unique position, as you will see.

While on leave I was recalled, and given orders to report to the Naval Base in Rota, even though I was not on alert. It was strange that I was not called back to Cartagena, since we are based in Algameca Naval Station. One other thing I noted was that the orders were issued by the Spanish Ministry of Defense, and contained only minimal information. As I heard later, many soldiers I knew (especially those in the Special Forces) also received such orders. Hugo, as well as my friends Neva Zapata, Jessenia Castillo, Miguel Ramos, Ben Zarco, Sebastián Valles, and several others in the armed forces, texted me soon after. Foreign soldiers I knew outside the country also messaged me from France, England, and Germany. It really seemed like everyone was being called up, all at once.

I had just started a vacation in Belgium at the time and had to fly home immediately. We had

9

been training very hard for the last year and I really was looking forward to some travel. The one thing I'll say is the cooler weather, for the short time I was in Brussels, was a really welcome change. Although I knew everything would eventually be explained, it was still annoying that I had my time off cancelled and had to rush back, gathering my things from the hotel and hastily boarding a morning flight. Anyway, it seemed like a chance to see some real action. Whatever was waiting, it was best not to dwell on it. Luckily, even in stressful situations I remain steady, and in those days I could fall asleep in minutes. Even though the flight was short, I remember closing the window shade and falling into a deep sleep as we rose through the clouds. Sometimes willful ignorance is, if not bliss, then a kind of irresponsible cocoon; a way to avoid the transformation that is coming.

Since I knew I'd probably be with Hugo, I had asked if he'd pick me up from the airport. He texted me back that he'd be waiting when I landed. I remember the plane touching down in Jerez and waking up annoyed. I just wanted to sleep a little longer but the most I could do was wait until nearly everyone had gotten their bags and disembarked. One flight attendant was giving me a thinly veiled bitch face, with angry eyes and a plastered smile. Maybe it had been a bad flight, I wouldn't know, but I think she wanted me to leave.

I slowly grabbed my pack and made my way to the front of the plane. As I exited and made my way up the ramp, I finally did what I had been delaying as long as possible – I turned my cellphone on. Notifications flooded in, especially from WhatsApp. Since I knew my time was running out, I sat in one of the first chairs near my gate. As the last of the passengers from my plane filed away, I allowed myself a few minutes of Candy Crush. I won two levels, but resisted the temptation to play a third. It was with a sigh that I started reading the messages and prepared to leave. I saw Hugo had texted, as well as Neva and Miguel. I sent some quick responses to let everyone knew I was back. Hugo immediately responded and said he'd pull up to the nearest exit. As I made my way through the airport, I looked up at the ceiling divided into large squares with little square windows lining each one. The bright morning light shone through and the airport was not even busy. I experienced a strange moment of infinite possibility, where I could have been coming or going, and allowed myself to wonder, if I left, where would I go?

Walking through the airport doors into the sunshine, I saw Hugo and waved. Of course he was parked nearly in front of the doors, where you're not supposed to be. He had been leaning against his old Ateca, deep in thought. The red paint was still in great shape as was the interior, although I still liked to tease him about its age to see if he'd ever buy a new car. Not that I think I had that amount of influence on him, but one never knows. He had a huge smile across his face and his neat, dark hair was perfectly blended into his rough stubble. He walked forward and we met in a firm embrace.

"Hugo! Thanks for coming to get me." I remember looking at him with my big, dumb smile. As we parted, our hands lingered on each other's sides, our fingertips gently squeezing each other. We had never done anything (we were both under the same command structure), and anyway we were both still young, with parents to look after and friends in common. But I couldn't stop myself from thinking...we wouldn't be in the military forever.

"Of course, Alba", he said earnestly.

"I do have to register a complaint - you still haven't got rid of this thing", I said motioning to the car. "I think Seat *does* make new models, right?"

He just laughed and said, "I never figured you for a materialist" at which I smiled and pretended to take great offense.

"It's not about material possessions, it's about whether our things reflect us in some way. Maybe I miss your old Seat 600. Somehow it was more you."

He straightened up and smiled, saying, "Well, if I could have kept it running..." He sighed. "Sometimes I wish I didn't have to be practical, but at least I'm dripping with modesty".

I just smiled and let it go. "Let's get something sweet", I said, "maybe flan"?

Hugo loudly pronounced, "No! To La Rosa de Oro! We'll get the palmeras de chocolates. I need some coffee too. Yes or yes?"

I said that sounded great and we threw my things in the back, before pulling away from the airport and getting on the A-4. Everything looked so green that day, maybe it was the light. We talked as I watched the scenery go by.

We parked as close as we could and walked down the pale blue and tan cobblestones of Calle Consistorio. There on the corner was an adjoined building - the left half was all uneven grey stone, as if carved out of solid rock, with large glass windows and on the right was a yellow stucco building. Over the door on the right a black sign with gold Art Nouveau lettering: "La Rosa de Oro". The interior was ochre and white, and in the front a glass case was filled with lovely pastries. We walked in and took a look, but we knew what we wanted.

I suggested we sit outside to people watch. It was a very pleasant day and we took our time, laughing about many good memories, but those I'll keep for myself. What I will share is that, when the timing was right, Hugo gave me a gift which he said could be of use on our deployment. In a box was a hand forged fixed-blade knife, like a very angular navaja. Sturdy and perfectly balanced, it feels natural in the hand. He had a nearly identical knife made for himself. On my blade is an inscription. This gift is a thing of beauty which I have always treasured.

When we were done, we headed for a narrow alley across the way. It was paved in blue, grey, and tan stones, but now in a checkerboard pattern. As we walked, the corridor of buildings enclosed us in a narrow embrace, most yellow or white stucco, some in stone, balconies hanging over each one, but no one there. The alley was completely empty. This opened up into a small square, so we headed left down another alley. This alley seemed even narrower, probably sized only for wagons. This eventually widened onto Calle Manuel Maria Gonzalez, with some beautiful plantings near Alameda Vieja appearing on our left. I still remember how clean it smelled that day.

The building on our right was a popular sherry bodega called Gonzalez Byass. As we walked along in conversation, there was an alley gate – green, with stone pillars, and all overgrown. On that day the gates were open, so we walked beneath that twining canopy of dark green grape leaves, the light filtering through to the cobbles, arranged into complex geometrics. I leaned against one of the white stucco walls, and asked poetically, "What's going to become of us?"

Hugo smiled, warm but faint, and turned toward me, resting his palm on the wall. "Whatever happens, we'll look out for each other".

Chapter 2

ROTA

Arriving at the car, we decided to really take our time getting back to base. We understood the hour was nearly at hand, ready for whatever was to come next, and there was no need to worry out loud. It is only the rare companion that one can share a comfortable silence with, even when you haven't run out of things to say. Hugo and I had decided to take a short nap in the car, then stop for drinks and tapas because…why not? The second we woke up though we both got a text from our commanding officer, Captain Carlos Gil, asking where we were. Carlos was a great leader, but intimidating – he was bald and built like an ox, with plenty of "don't fuck with me" vibes. He was also probably the only person I knew more closed off than myself, yet somehow he was an extrovert. We were not far from the station but were careful to tell as little as possible. Hugo texted back "In transit, be there in an hour". We had a little laugh over that but decided to be good and make our way to NAVSTA Rota. Leaving Jerez de la Frontera, we drove down the A-480 with its little rolling hills and fields. As the green landscape slid past under a clear blue sky, we listened to (and fought over) music. Hugo insisted on playing Orchestra Baobab, which had actually grown on me, but I insisted on not telling him. As we got into Rota, we drove around aimlessly for a little while to claw back the remainder of our hour. We saw a silver sculpture of two hands reaching toward the sky in a roundabout, drove by the ocean, and eventually had to make our way back to the base despite some minor traffic. Nothing accomplished; it was worth every moment.

Pulling into the entrance we were surprised by the number of vehicles in our way. Ahead we saw the familiar gate across the road, plain white stucco with red tile roof, but the number of vehicles clogging the way in front of us was something we had never seen. The cacophony of noise and unexpected commotion was something we should have anticipated, but I think we were deliberately enjoying a moment of lovely ignorance. Hugo pulled in and we grabbed our bags. I took a deep breath and we set out to find a CPO Jimenez, as directed. The normally relaxed vibes at NAVSTA Rota were gone, replaced by an electric energy, not frantic, but insistent.

Jimenez saw us walking and paced over, calling our names. "Good Afternoon. There is another briefing that has just started. I'll take you to the hangar. Follow me." Hugo and I just looked at each other, since they could have briefed us inside, maybe in a conference room or the auditorium; we had been there before. We tried to get more information from Jimenez but he wouldn't budge. It was a relatively mild day, but the sun was still beating down on us as we took the long, silent walk over to a large blue and white hangar. As we got out of the sun onto the cool, Caribbean blue floor shaded by the well lit metal roof of the hangar, we saw a number of plastic chairs set up in front of a series of folding tables laid end to end. CPO Jimenez gestured to the chairs and saw himself out. Only about half the seats were filled, so we sat toward the front. I didn't recognize any of the five faces seated at the head table, but I saw some of my teammates in the audience after I sat down. Of those at the table, the man at the center was a clean cut US Navy Lieutenant Commander named Bauer. Commander Bauer was talking quietly to those on his left and right, white cap bobbing up and down as he made some last minute points to his colleagues. As to who all those colleagues were, I am still not sure, as they were never introduced. The man to his immediate right was our own Vice Admiral Aguirre Cañadas, followed by FGNE Commander Colonel De León. Further right was a calm man in an understated suit - he said nothing. To Commander Bauer's left were, I felt, both a French and a German man. I was guessing they were intelligence since they were wearing suits. I guessed their nationality based on demeanor and accent.

Commander Bauer turned back to us and stared us down, "Alright, let's get started since I'll probably be called away soon. I'd like to welcome you to the start of what will be the greatest test many of you will ever face, but great things have modest beginnings. So I'll try to explain as simply as I can. America is at war, and recently we have been calling for "intervention upon invitation" in this time of need. We've been working to get United Nations support. We are now successful, finally, after complex negotiations, in invoking Article Five of the NATO Charter. There had been enough interference before, from both China and Russia, to say that a foreign adversary had, in part, created the current crisis. As such, Spain and all the other members of NATO are activating a massive push to help defeat the terrorist insurgency in the US and restore order. NATO's Very High Readiness Joint Task Force and Response Forces will be activated as a spearhead but not immediately, since this will take planning. A larger force will follow.

The enemy consists of various local militias and a well-armed countrywide insurgent group called the Patriots. The Patriots are well led, with many of our own military officers defecting to their ranks. The leader of the Patriots is the former Vice Chairman of the Joint Chiefs of Staff, General O'Connor. He is committing treason by levying war against the United States. We will handle him when he's caught. General Spencer is the number two man. Now, General Spencer's location is unknown but we think he's in the Deep South, which will be a major operation. We'll make a decision on capture whether we can safely try him in the US. Your mission is to capture O'Connor's third in command, General Douglas Hahn, which takes out their three most capable commanders. Due to the danger of keeping these folks in America, we'll split the difference and go through Spain on this particular mission, which will rely on universal jurisdiction. There have been dozens of documented cases of Spanish Nationals having been murdered by the Patriots and aligned militias. This gives Spain the legal right to investigate and prosecute. To avoid further danger Spanish Nationals have been evacuated from Texas, New Mexico and other states to California when requested, and repatriated to Spain. The NSA has intercepted numerous orders by General Hahn himself to 'liquidate' whole residential areas and even cities. Those orders tie directly to the deaths in question. We will turn over all evidence to Spain at the proper time."

I asked "Why not Germany, which also has universal jurisdiction?"

"There are other operations", the German man said with restrained annoyance.

Captain Bauer said, "Agreed. The Franco-German brigade is headed to the Deep South. By trying General O'Connor in the US and trying General Hahn abroad, the two methods should show both solidarity and the inescapability of justice. Turkey, Greece, and a few other countries are only going to provide token forces, so the bulk of the soldiers will be French, German, British, Spanish, Italian, Polish, Canadian, and Dutch, who will join a major American push and fan out from the Mid-Atlantic into the Deep South, all the way down, until we push to the Atlantic shorelines - from Louisiana clear over to Florida. Somewhere down there we'll capture General Spencer, who might be tried in Germany. This ought to cement NATO ties; show that we're all on the same page, we're in this together, and there's nowhere to hide. We need to take out the Patriot leadership, roll up the die-hards, and restore stability. We have CIA folks assigned to help every one of your teams in any capacity they… can. Sorry…" Captain Bauer stopped and looked down at the very phone call he had mentioned at the start, which he said he *had* to take. Muting the call for a moment, he left us with a final direction: "Talk to The Agency folks in the other building, they'll get you up to speed. Dismissed". With that he left, his face focused only on his call.

After Captain Bauer and two of the others left the head table, a few of us from FGNE stayed behind, not quite sure what we even wanted to say or ask. Vice Admiral Aguirre Cañadas had remained in his seat and appraised us without saying anything, likewise the silent man to his right. Cañadas lit up a cigar and raised it to his hardened face. He took a puff and held it casually aside in his right hand, "Call me Javier. You'll have about 6 months to soak up intel, train, and prepare. Don't waste it. Go meet up with the various Special Forces groups here and compare notes. I want you to soak everything up, and then improve on it. The US is supporting everything we're doing, including with funding."

Hugo asked, "So does that mean we can customize whatever we need?"

Javier leaned in and slowly raised his hands, palm facing each other, for emphasis. "I will make sure you have whatever weapons, modifications, and equipment you need. Just tell the support units, or procure items and we'll reimburse you. As I said, the Americans will be helping in any way they can, by providing funding, material, intelligence, and training. If there is any gap discovered in training, we may be able to offer custom technical solutions. There's a big push to activate and combine all useful research and development, from both Europe and America. Let me be clear, we are going to war *in the United States of America*, until now the most powerful nation on the face of the earth. Maximizing your dexterity, equipment, operational flexibility, and experience is the *bare minimum* necessary to achieve victory. So if you feel you need something, anything, the answer is yes. Push as hard as you need to in America, and let *nothing* stop you."

Carlos simply said, "Yes Sir!"

Keeping fierce eye contact, the Vice Admiral brought his hands down rather heavily on the table and said, "Plus Ultra." With that, the Vice Admiral tilted his head a little while puffing his cigar, regarding us again. Without breaking eye contact, he exhaled, nodded once, and excused himself after reminding us to go see Tim from CIA. The other gentleman with him got up at the same time and left as well, saying nothing. They simply walked off behind some helicopters and out of sight.

Carlos said he had a different meeting to go to, but directed the teams on where they should report and to whom. Hugo, Neva, Miguel, and I set out with some others to the next building to find Tim just as we had been told and asked a soldier there for directions to the right room.

Chapter 3

THE AGENCY

We knocked and entered a cluttered
conference room, which was fairly large but littered
with papers and equipment. They asked us to leave
the door open. These people had clearly
commandeered the room as a makeshift
headquarters. There were several whiteboards,
which now seemed to cover any available wall
space. Tim was with the Central Intelligence
Agency's Special Operations Group and he was
accompanied by an analyst named Nicole. We all
shook hands and introduced each other. Tim was
average height but strong, with dark skin,
noticeably thinning hair, and tired but honest eyes
that seemed to look concerned even when his face
was at rest. Nicole was almost gaunt, with curly
light brown hair, an easy smile, and such thin hands.
For that reason, every time I shook her hand I tried
to be gentle. She also looked tired that day but her
demeanor was always cheery and inquisitive. We
would get to know them well during our time there,
and they offered us so many insights that I don't
think we could have ever repaid them.

Tim asked if we were marines, and then
offered this joke: "The Army and Navy are military,
the Air Force is corporate, and the Marines are a
cult".

Hugo and I both said, "Hey…" then looked at each other and laughed.

Tim laughed too, and threw his hands up defensively, "No disrespect, I'm not going to accuse you guys of eating *crayons* or anything like that… unlike those other branches. They *definitely* think you eat crayons…but The Agency prides itself on being professional" he finished cheerily.

I immediately raised my right hand to halt him and shot back, "I'm glad you'd never. Good relationships are built on trust…so, if you leave a few crayons out for us, we'll get along just fine."

Tim cracked a smile but regained his composure and held up three fingers, "Three crayons, no red ones".

I snapped into negotiation mode, "Five, two red".

Tim just crossed his arms, turned his head to the side, nose turned up, and sniffed in mock indignation after a dramatic pause, "No deal".

"No deal? Maybe I should join the CIA instead. I feel like I'm already under cover, because you're putting me to sleep."

Hugo tried to hold in his smirk. Tim turned his head back, his mouth agape, then started to laugh. Nicole snorted through her nose. Neva and Miguel joined in, and we all had a good laugh.

"Ok, I like this group." Tim said he was glad we could all break the ice, especially since we'd be working closely over the next few months. It was important we got on well. He took on a sterner tone

24

and said, "I want to spend the next week just briefing you guys on what's happening in America: the who, what, when, where, why, and how. Understanding is the key to taking any meaningful action – understanding our enemies, the situation, and ourselves. That's how we'll win, and that's why I'll be briefing all of the key operators. We'll have some presentations of course, but it's always quicker to get up to speed in a question and answer environment. You'll need that edge because this is a huge undertaking, not some peacekeeping mission"

He continued, "Most people can't agree on when this became a civil war, and for a while we couldn't all agree whether that's what it even was. This isn't as clear-cut as the first civil war, with a large contiguous group of Southern states seceding from the Union. There is a subtext of regionalism, racism and anti-establishment thinking which ironically seems to be authoritarian in nature. With all that said, the South is still going to be the most difficult region"

Nicole interjected, as she often does in her excited way, "It does seem like a contradiction that all of these groups want to both destroy authority for having too much power, and yet create something more authoritarian. Most groups say they just want to be left alone with no government interference, but most of them also seem to want to be the final law of the land. They want control of our symbology and culture, while cloaking themselves in libertarianism. The whole thing would make for a fascinating sociological study".

Tim went on, "Attacks by lone wolves and militia members started years ago but the last election, which the right wing had changed laws to try to rig, was where it got a lot worse. The pace and severity of attacks increased as time went on. Some people blame the Taiwan War, but we won that."

At this point, Hugo asked, "but did you?"

Tim said, "I take your point, but whose navy is on the bottom of the Pacific? Well, who has *more* ships on the bottom at least. China overplayed their hand too soon, that's why they pulled back. Same with Russia in Ukraine. That's partly what made the Taiwan War more limited than we expected, they fought alone. I know the Russians are more wary of the CCP now, plus they're trying to fix their own system after the coup, so they're staying home and doing the only thing they need to do – stop causing chaos. At least the psychotronic attacks have fallen silent. Plus it takes pressure off Europe. It's good we stood up to them over Ukraine early on, otherwise appeasement may have emboldened them. Fuck the Restraint IR school, am I right? China is also in a weaker position than it was, especially with their demographics. There's no doubt all of that mess plus interference from the Russians and the Chinese contributed greatly to our troubles, but you know propaganda – you have to have flaws and fractures to begin with. We've kept in contact with them, and with all world leaders to provide assurance that our nuclear arsenal is safe and will remain that way.

"Anyway, for me, I think I'd draw the line for the start of the US conflict as a true civil war before most of the House and Senate had been murdered, before the defections from cops and soldiers, to when the Secretary of State was murdered in Texas. When that happened, a radical immediately replaced them, and partisan judges let that violence go. Judges had been doing that a lot actually, but it got *real* political. The Supreme Court also made a lot of hack political decisions that helped precipitate the violence. Vigilantism is ok; Rule of Law depends on which side you're on, State's Rights as a way to undermine Federal Authority and make sure no one is accountable... you get the picture.

Yes, the left wing did protest, some people did get violent, and some of the protests damaged property. The prior President responded with the help of his folks in Congress, trying to establish a fully authoritarian government, similar to Russia, including the part where they get rich. States had been exempting themselves from Federal law for years. The new golden rule was: "Help your friends, hurt your enemies". No one had a clear answer to it. It was hard enough to get the arrest in that Texas case, which happened only due to the public outcry. To see the case almost summarily dismissed due to political affinity and moral cowardice...well that pretty much ate up any remaining trust in the Judicial Branch. It was like they had someone already waiting in the wings prior to the assassination. As the Tao Te Ching says, 'When the country is confused and in chaos, loyal ministers appear'. I think of that as the beginning, since it was far more explicit than a wink and a nod. I mean, they were basically saying "you can come and try to take this power from my cold, dead hands; I'm keeping it".

Many folks from the far right praised the violence and seemed fine with the subsequent impunity from the rule of law, although they framed it as restoring the law. Maybe they needed to express their feelings with action. As many people have said, sometimes the cruelty *is* the point. Many on the very far left seemed to be almost hoping for the inevitable chaos they knew would follow. I guess they never factored in where they'd get their morning latte, or the fact that communism is when all the means of production are owned by one dictator's mustache. That was about two and a half..."

At which point Tim paused and looked to Nicole, who finished, "two years and nine months ago".

Tim nodded and went on, "Then, the presidential election a couple years ago, and complete meltdown. He proposed a number of changes to make the US more democratic, which was despised by the right. After several more cases of violence and terrorism mostly being punished only in states that voted for the new president, state laws were passed to essentially whitewash vigilantism. Conservative judges upheld those same laws with a laissez-faire attitude to violence. That's when things really deteriorated. So basically, it was the judges who fucked us."

Then Nicole added some detail, "At first the militias were just *threatening* violence and carrying guns everywhere, but it turned physical. They were beating up liberals, people of color, Jews, gays, intellectuals, and even media figures. This was especially true in more liberal places like LA. It's not like this was at protests either, just people walking down the street or shopping in stores. Real Kristallnacht vibes, but over many months. So, like, Kristalljahr. Being Jewish, I'd rate the last decade as one star, would not do again. In California at least, the high number of arrests for domestic terrorism and hate crimes diminished the violence. Arresting the worst offenders nationwide did work for a little while, but their leaders kept stirring up more violence in new places. They were treated more lightly every year by the justice system in many states, and had a lot of sympathizers. Sympathizers to 'extremism in the defense of liberty' and all that. People would threaten those who talked. Eventually sympathizers stopped helping the cops, so these crimes got harder to solve. In many cases cops were also sympathizers."

Tim inhaled and said, "Yeah also, in a divided culture, the more troublemakers you arrest, the more you may turn their family, friends, and neighbors against you. So there's that. What we *should* have done was arrest those in congress who were essentially using stochastic terrorism for years with no accountability. That's how the lack of accountability by political leaders, and moral cowardice by those who should uphold the rule of law caused systemic failure. Lead by example my ass, they were some of the biggest children! Like I said, that includes the Judicial Branch and even Law Enforcement. No one wanted to arrest a congressperson as a terrorist, or a judge for subverting the rule of law. Whether left or right, it was the little guy that always took the fall. No one wanted to arrest *anyone* for treason, no matter *what* they did. Suddenly it was, 'oh, well that law hasn't been used in X years'. I'm sorry, but what the fuck! Is it not still law? So if there are a couple of years without murders, the murder laws no longer apply? Fuck outta here. It was all weakness and stupidity. Typical…American…weakness. Things went on way too long before we even tried to *halfway* deal with any core issues. In other words, we did what we always do: throw the dead bodies behind the drywall and wallpaper over it. Ignore the stench." Tim took a deep breath and threw up both hands, "Sorry, I'm ranting. Anyway, once militias started to use actual terrorism like bombings and assassinations to make their point, then of course the government got harsher. Did they go too far sometimes? Maybe. That only encouraged the militias to step up their attacks. That led to more arrests, harsher treatment, deeper political division, and the cycle continued. Right wing nationalist militias were just splinter groups by themselves but difficult to completely defeat because they were everywhere, and growing. With all the collateral damage, overstep, and regionalism, random people started to join the militias, or splinter into their own thing. The more we fought, the worse things got. The economy tanked of course.

"Then the worst of it began. There had always been a lot of veterans joining militias, but then active duty folks started going AWOL. No doubt veterans were in their ear trying to peel them away. At first we just found them and court-martialed them, but as numbers increased finding them started to get harder and harder. They'd hide in the woods or get help from locals. These former and active duty soldiers and cops started to merge their interests with the civilian militias while still keeping some separation. The worst for those of us who remained loyal was the internal threats, the anonymous notes and messages from co-workers. You knew they could tip off the militias and get you or your family killed at any time. Not all militias, but many, hold hard-core racist and fascist beliefs. This might have been a bit more unpalatable for some of the right wing military folks who seemed to be holding out for fascism lite. Then again, maybe

they were just waiting for an excuse, or a rallying
point. Unfortunately, along came the Patriots, lead
by General O'Connor. He acted as the catalyst.
High-level brass started to retire shortly after he did,
while involving themselves with the far-right
movement. They also courted those on the far-left
who wanted to tear down the current system. While
the Patriots started small, he knew just what to say
to rile everyone up and get them on-side. His
personality is apparently enough to hold it all
together. The violence got a lot worse - more brazen
and cruel. He'd keep just enough distance in public
while being involved behind the scenes. He had this
air of impunity, and since no one seemed willing to
do anything real like arrest him, the impunity
became real. The bigger he talked, the more people
joined. Once they gained enough members, active
duty military started not just defecting, but stealing
equipment. We had folks driving off with JLTVs,
flying off with bombers, and stealing artillery,
supplies, gunboats. The Patriots moved with
precision to take as much as they could early on,
before we tried our best to slam the door shut. I
would say that a quarter of the armed services and
equipment was taken and a lot of the rest sabotaged.
They even managed to keep moles in every
department, and every branch of Government. They
stayed on to disinform and gather intel; disgusting.
Of police, I think the percent of white officers
who've quit or become active against the
government is about *a third*. Let that shit sink in. A

third of white police officers, when the time came, chose to leave or stab our country, and their own communities, in the back. This is part of why we've had such a hard time trying to regain authority. I guess they felt their community was defined a little different than how we'd define it. So the President declared martial law. That brings us to the final nail in the coffin."

Nicole chimed in, "Texas!"

Tim went on, "We think Texas is about to secede. There has always been chatter among militias, and big talk from everyone else, but this is different. The governor has been very coy, and we notice how Texas sees less of the violence, but militia members seem to be using it as a home base, moving in and out to attack neighboring states. This seems to be with the tacit support of the Governor. We've been sending convoys through there when we can to make sure there are no surprises, but they've started hassling any military they see - basic area denial stuff. There are also an unusual number of Texans who've run off to join the Patriots, or disappeared entirely. So, our intel says it's likely just a matter of time. We think they're playing a double game and I'm not sure we can afford another war in the middle of this one. On the other hand, they seem to be dragging this conflict out with the promise of making it worse after secession. So we have to watch the clock, we don't have long. We've already moved a lot of assets and loyal soldiers to

California, just to be on the safe side and project power from the West."

Neva asked, "How do you know who's loyal?"

Tim said, "We took a look at social media, vaccine hesitancy, a bunch of different clues. Recently we've been trying to step up lie detector tests for new recruits; very targeted questions.

"The US military is still holding key sites, such as nukes and most bases, although we've had to abandon some. We control the Northeast, Delmarva, southern FL, and a lot of the West. From California we've defeated militia in much of Eastern Oregon, Washington, Colorado, and Western New Mexico. We still have ongoing conflicts in Idaho, Nevada, Utah, and most other Western states, but it's not as concentrated as the East Coast. Climate Change is really kicking our ass too. A lot of the power grid keeps going down. Texas's grid is shaky, but the Western Grid, and most of the Northeast, is doing better at keeping the lights on. Here too, Texas seems to be trying to undermine nearby states with propaganda about their power being on while secretly helping those who cause outages elsewhere.

"So this is where you come in, as part of NATO and the Multi-National Force. NATO will land on the East Coast, meeting at Joint Force Command Norfolk. This will lighten the load on US forces and we should be able to re-exert control. The US will provide Spain and the rest of NATO forces with additional arms, money, training, and intelligence. We're glad that your country has already nearly doubled military spending in recent years, and it shows. We plan to increase our financial assistance so you can make any difficult choices a little easier. I've heard the King is very much in favor of the mission, so I think you'll have all the backing you need. Why not get some chow and rest, we can talk more tomorrow."

As we were getting up Neva asked, "So if we need to find you, are you two usually in this room?"

Tim said, "Yes, we are literally sleeping in here" as he gestured to two narrow cots with sleeping bags set up in the corner behind the long table, which was piled so high with books, files and papers we hadn't even seen them there.

Getting up from the table, amidst the clutter I noticed a tiny copy of the book he had quoted to us – the Tao Te Ching. I majored in Philosophy so remember having to read it in college, but figured it would be an interesting way to unwind before bed. "Hey Tim" I asked, holding it up, "do you mind if I borrow this for the night?"

"Sure", he said. "As a matter of fact, you keep it, I have another copy."

I thanked him for letting me have his book and put it in my pocket. Hugo, Miguel, Neva and I all shook hands with Tim and Nicole, and thanked them before starting to leave. Neva let out a little gasp and a "*¡Joder!*" under her breath. I turned and saw the same man that had been sitting next to Vice Admiral Cañadas now sitting in a chair against the wall. His grey-on-beige outfit may as well have been made as a Ghillie suit for office environments; an invisible man for the modern age. Even his haircut was too normal – a slightly receding hairline met brown hair of nondescript length all combed to the side. I don't even know when he came in. He looked at us calmly but said nothing, apparently waiting to speak to Tim and Nicole. As we filed out, Hugo asked Tim if he should shut the door just as we saw another CIA officer exiting from the next room with several more of my fellow soldiers. As he shut the door, the other group walked away, down the hall and made a turn. I wondered how many more conversations like ours were happening, and in how many other rooms.

Miguel spoke up, "He seems like a good dude, what do you guys think?"

Neva looked at me and said, "Well, Alba got a free book out of it, so he's ok by me".

I couldn't disagree. We all decided to go the café to talk and finally get something to eat (other than MREs). The discussion was what America would be like. It sounded like absolute chaos, and I didn't really feel like we were going to solve anything that night. I had some fruit and a couple pieces of awful pizza that tasted like trash. I ate quick, saying that I was tired and just wanted to read for a bit. Hugo quietly asked if I was ok, and I reassured him I was fine.

We all went back to our rooms in the barracks, which was great because we had some say over our roommates. I chose Neva as my roommate, but I recall Jessenia always being in our room too, flopping her curly dark hair around like she does. Inquisitive and curious, she was a good soldier, but a bit too open sometimes. She was forever trying to get our read on different men she was interested in, which was frankly exhausting, but of course we loved her anyway.

That night I remember bringing my things into the room, laying down, closing the door, and reading the entire Tao Te Ching from cover to cover. It spoke to me a lot more than the first time I had read it, maybe because I had grown older, I don't know. I seemed to understand it better, and could dimly see that there was a lot more under the surface of the words, all kinds of implications. Neva tried to come in and have a conversation about what I thought was going to happen in America, but I just wanted to lie in the dark and think, so I wished her good night and thought about everything and nothing. I knew that what would sharpen me was not just military practices, but the heuristics I chose in thinking through problems, the frameworks I used for understanding. I remember sleeping like a stone that night, completely unworried.

Chapter 4

Day 2, Morning

When we woke up the next morning I let Neva take a shower and flipped through the Tao again. I had some breakfast and put some things away while waiting for the bathroom. After she was done and I had already jumped in the shower, Hugo came to our room. I heard him knock a couple of times on our door. Neva answered and I could hear her flirting a bit, even though I couldn't hear what was said. I heard her footsteps and a knock on the bathroom as she came in.

She called out, "Hey! Alba, we have another meeting with Tim. Apparently it's a lot more people today, different room. You know, Hugo asked how you were doing. What's up with you two anyway?"

"Ugh, we're just friends!" I was just trying to take my shower in peace.

"So you don't mind if I talk to him?" I didn't answer. "Yeah, that's what I thought. All I'm saying is I see how you look at him. You're not that sly Alba. You know, the things you regret the most are the things you never do."

I sighed, "Neva, advice not asked for, advice poorly heard. I just want to get ready. Nothing's going on between us. Besides I don't want to get in trouble, or ruin…"

"Ok" she said, cutting me off, "but I'm watching you!"

She practically skipped off to her room, surely please with herself. She can be so annoying sometimes, but she's always a great friend. I finished getting ready and we headed down to see Tim, but apparently this meeting was in a much larger room. We just followed everyone else.

I filed into the auditorium and sat down next to Neva, but I didn't recognize all of the soldiers sitting around me. There were some soldiers from Bétera I recognized nearby, from the NATO Rapid Deployable Corps I think. Hugo and Miguel were sitting a couple of rows ahead of us. After a few more minutes Tim introduced himself and said he wanted to get started. People kept filing in until there was standing room only. He looked up toward Nicole, who was running the projector, to start a slide deck. The screen simply showed a welcome.

Tim jumped right in, "If I can have everyone's attention…thanks. Normally I'd lead the discussion myself, but since he's here, my boss is going to give you all an overview of the war so far. Frank?"

This Frank was a tough older man with buzzed gray hair, clean cut, and no nonsense. He didn't waste any time with introductions or preamble. I do remember he started with a question: "I know you all might think you know what America might be like when you get there…so, what do you want to know?" No one said anything, so he asked again, "Anyone?"

Miguel raised his hand and asked, "I hear there are child soldiers, is that true?

Frank explained, "There *are* children who are acting as soldiers in militias, often along with their family, so the answer is yes, but they aren't typically pressed into service like in some other conflicts we've seen".

Neva blurted out "What about mass killings? We've heard about rape and torture and other things."

Frank did not flinch, honestly admitting there had been a number of recorded atrocities, and that part of our job would be to charge those responsible with war crimes, if we could prove it. "Everything that you think might go on in a brutal civil war is happening. Civilians are always in great danger in those areas we don't control. There have been killings, maiming, rapes, torture…when an enemy militia manages to overcome an impromptu neighborhood defense force, they'll often kill many of the adults, especially males. I've heard that some militias have taken any remaining children back to their camps, to do what with we can only guess. The situation is so fragile, so fractious; it's not usually possible to send people in undercover, for instance. This is an ugly, in your face kind of conflict. Firefights in the US are rarely over 500 meters, probably more like 25m-300m. There is also a lot of close quarters violence. In fact, this brings us to my single slide: War Crimes.

Frank asked Nicole to move on to his slides, which were really just dark grey bullet points on a white background. Much of this was reiteration for most of us, but he said we were going to have far more autonomy, carrying out a mission with a vast scope, and we needed to be self-directed by the rule of law. I found the topic fascinating because I almost decided to go to law school, but opted for a philosophy degree...of course, then I ended up in the military. Frank continued on to explain how war crimes must be in service of the conflict, as differentiated from a simple murder (such as for personal gain). The crime must also be a serious violation of international humanitarian law, not some petty crime like stealing. Most important, war crimes are on the head of the individual – there's no collective you can use to shirk your duties as a human being, sloughing your responsibility off onto a group's decision. Examples of war crimes, which we ourselves were also explicitly forbidden from carrying out, were murder, torture, mutilation, taking hostages, intentional attacks against civilians, and intentional attacks against important cultural landmarks like churches, schools, museums, historical monuments or hospitals. More examples include pillaging, rape, conscription of children under 15, or unlawful confinement. Frank advised us of our responsibilities, and how to gather and retain evidence of war crimes to be used later on.

War Crimes must be prosecuted in other countries with universal jurisdiction, such as Spain. So we'd need to set up a consistent, large-scale means of trying all of these crimes, and work with France, Germany, and the Netherlands to arrive at the rules of these tribunals. At the end of his presentation, he made the point that the very chaos that we were there to extinguish would invite expediency or rage, and we would inevitably lose people, so therefore we needed to always follow the law of armed conflict. I remember the last thing he said before he opened it up to a question and answer. He looked out at the crowd, and with total conviction, simply said, "Do you know what this war is about? It's about justice. Never forget that".

Now the questions came, with many others raising their hands. A soldier in the back asked, "Is it true the president was assassinated and the military is actually in charge?"

"No. That's horseshit. Not to say folks haven't tried, but it's propaganda. The president is alive and well in California."

The same man asked a follow-up, "So did California try to secede?"

"No. California is still very much a part of the United States, as are all the other states. The problem is we have a number of folks who *think* they might be able to secede, or form their own sovereign communities, which they can't. We have moved the temporary capital West to California. The Western half of the US is less densely populated overall, so we can safely project power Eastward as we retake everything else. I'm not gonna lie, we've lost a lot of ground, including some military bases, entire cities, and huge swaths of the country. That's not to say that all of the citizens in those areas are against us, but they certainly can't do much other than survive and steer clear of trouble.

Someone asked the next logical question, "Is Texas seceding?"

At this Frank paused a moment, then carefully said, "No. So far they are still a state; technically the same as all the rest. In all honesty they seem to be toying with the idea. We have to be very careful, because after all these little militias, and now the Patriots, the last thing we need is Texas seceding. That would be a war within a war within a war. I'll just say they do seem to be making some moves, in case they can take advantage in some way."

"Since you're asking about individual states, I'll try to do a quick overview. The West Coast is safer, especially California. Initially we had lots of terrorist attacks in Cali, but we crushed any kind of armed resistance, knowing these terrorists would selfishly sink the whole experiment if they succeeded. We needed somewhere to operate from given the resistance and high population on the East Coast. We had to put down some heavy resistance in Washington and Oregon. We've brought those states back to a near-normal though, other than natural disasters and rooting out terrorism. Idaho, Montana, and Wyoming we're keeping forces very centralized to respond to emergencies. That area will need a very light touch for now. Even though the population is low, the secessionists are riding high for now. The Western half of the US, as I said, is less populated, so we basically fight and feed people as needed. We're not trying to get everyone to agree on everything per se, just to coexist: to stop killing each other.

The fight goes on in the West, since there are still regions heavily against us. Alaska is not actually one of them. We've been in steady contact with them from Cali, and we've even sent some more troops in case any foreign country gets ideas. Fort Greely has been on high alert, for instance. Most of the folks in Alaska can hunt and fish, and their electric grid is holding up. They've got plenty of natural gas, hydro, and renewables. We keep them supplied with the things they don't have, so they're fine. Any terrorists up there, we deal with by police action. As I said, the West is doing better than the East.

We still have control of the Northeast, although there are still numerous attacks there. It's really bad from the mid-Atlantic and especially throughout the South. All the opposition forces realize that if they can seize control of the mid-Atlantic region, they'll have a lot of ability to project power. The Midwest is another area where we've had huge problems. The Eastern interior is actually all pretty rough, and in a lot of places, kind of apocalyptic. The lack of electricity combined with storms plus the violence has left some places a hell-scape. As I said, the South is a complete fucking mess, and will have to be the focus of a major push.

Texas has kept its grid on most of the time and kept people a lot safer from some of the militia violence, but that's partly because there's a lot of sympathy for it there too. For nearby states, this makes Texas a popular destination to retreat from the madness, if folks can make it that far. Unfortunately, it also seems like a popular place for terrorists, like the militias and Patriots, to hide out from the fighting. And I can't say Texas has been remotely helpful in apprehending them, claiming all kinds of state's rights. It's like Cambodia and Laos during Vietnam. They seem to relish their position, and it wouldn't surprise me if they try to secede at the worst possible time." Frank stopped after a few more questions and turned it over to Nicole.

Nicole took us through a kind of statistician's wet dream of a slide deck. There were polls, charts, and graphs, and county level multi-year voting results, and topographic maps, and militia territory maps. There were lots of maps…so many maps. Interestingly, she did start with why these people *said* were fighting: much of it was horseshit, similar to the first US Civil War. There were so many conspiracy theories throughout the general population, plus a tangle of fear, anger, and greed, mixed with a broken system, that it seemed like it would be a herculean effort to restore reason. Amidst that, I heard a lot of genuine drivers like AI and automation leading to job losses, the destruction of the middle class, the power of the wealthy (who had hired private armies to protect them), unchecked violence from all sides, and government complacency. She continued, "We're trying to use food diplomacy to maintain some semblance of civilization, but for everything we try to repair, like the electric grid, terrorism takes it back out." She went through all the data around the frequent terror attacks, which states and cities were worst off, and where we would likely be needed. The next slides were about climate change, and recent storms, fires, and floods that had damaged many regions. It was critical to know these things, but I think by the end of the deck we all felt a little dead inside.

When we broke for lunch Hugo actually headed over to Frank before he could leave, asking him what the President's plans were for the country, after the war. Frank seemed impressed by the question and was brutally honest. He said the President thought that certain flaws in the system, combined with a poor understanding of the responsibilities of any government, allowed us to fall prey to internal stresses that were made worse through external conflicts. The plan was to restructure the US Government so that it would endure for a thousand years, thanks to its *system*, not to luck and the whims of powerful men (which was always a bullshit gamble). The restructuring would proscriptively drive greater progress, cohesion, and collaboration. The US was going to double down on Democracy.

Hugo replied, "So the cult of the individual over the group, and the cult of the group over the individual, both need to die".

Then Frank just grabbed his coffee, slapping Hugo on the arm as he was turning and said, "Yeah, but first we have to win the war. Time for lunch."

Chapter 5

Day 2, Afternoon

The expectation was that the Americans
would serve inadequate pizza and cola. We were all
surprised to find they had catering brought in from a
couple of great local restaurants. To say we took our
time was an understatement, and all of the lively
conversation re-energized us (that and the coffee)
When we came back, Frank was already at the
podium shuffling through papers. We all filed in
feeling quite satisfied with lunch. He looked up
over his reading glasses and said, "All right Nicole,
you want to get back into the slides?" A sigh passed
through the audience.

"Sure, thanks. Ok, a little change of pace
here…let's talk about training." A sigh of relief
passed through the audience. With that, Nicole put
up a single slide that said: "What's the Plan?" "You
have about six months, and we want to give you as
much data as we can this week, but after that we
know you'll be training hard. The basic plan is to
cross train, given the number of Special Forces we
have here from several countries. We also had the
idea to cover different cycles of training, such as
SERE, with multiple classes at different times. This
would maximize training so everyone is trained on
everything. There are some courses we've already
decided on, but we'd be glad to listen to any ideas

you have. Since he was usually so quiet, I was surprised to hear Sebastián speak up to ask a question, "Nicole, is it possible to shift locations to different terrains? I've been to America before. It's a big country with lots of different landscapes. It would be good experience to find similar settings to train at."

Frank, Tim, and Nicole looked at each other. Frank offered an answer, "Probably. We'd need to work out the logistics and the cost, but I agree. It's a good idea. Let me make sure it's ok and I'll get back to you all."

Nicole asked if anyone else had any ideas, especially for what we felt we would like more training on. She asked that we introduce ourselves before speaking and pulled up a spreadsheet on screen to record ideas. There were soldiers from several countries in attendance and they all produced some good ideas. Three Green Berets gave their thoughts first, offering ideas in quick succession. They introduced themselves as they talked. Dave, Noah, and Ben (who we came to call the beards) threw LandNav out as an idea, followed by SERE, MOS, combatives, small unit tactics, urban combat, guerrilla warfare, bush craft, language, acclimation to different terrains, and lastly some kind of Robin Sage type exercise, perhaps at the end. This was such a thorough list we sat there while Nicole typed it up in the first column so we could see if there was anything to add. A man named David, from Sayeret Matkal (which is an

Israeli special Forces unit) made a couple of very direct points about using what was tried and true, essentially training to perfectly execute the basics. There was someone from French COS named Phillipe who was a bit opinionated, but made a good counterpoint to David, which is that we should not be afraid to try new things, or find new ways. I saw a very solid operator I knew, named Jack, from the SAS. We had worked together before on a training exercise in the UK and I recognized him across the auditorium by his dark scruffy hair. He backed up David's point about executing on the basics, but also wanted to make sure we were picking up the *right* skills that we'd actually need and use in America.

A SEAL Team member named Mike offered counterterrorism, reconnaissance, and hostage rescue. This was a very alpha guy, but his voice cracked a little, and he said, "Whatever we do we better do it right, because I lost friends…". With that he choked up and couldn't go any further, ending it with "Sorry, sorry". An Army Ranger named Dan joined in sadly, "Agreed. I've lost…a lot of men. And I just want America back. You know? We can't fail. That's it." With that he ended, rubbing his eyes.

Frank pulled off his reading glasses and stepped in to steady things, "God damn right. We will not fail. It is victory, and no other option. The President has been clear: once we pacify the country, the restructuring of government will prevent this from *ever* happening again. No one will have died in vain. I can assure you of that."

Another man raised his hand and introduced himself by his first name, which I will not add here, and said that he was in the CIA's Special Activities Center, Ground Branch. "I'd like to add surveillance, trade craft, advanced driving, tracking, electronic warfare, and kidnapping. Hopefully everyone will cross train on everything. Most of these folks should be able to move quickly into advanced training, and I know we don't want injuries. An element of randomness mixed with standardized modules and plenty of PT would work well here. For instance, combatives every morning, but maybe like a mini-SERE day, or room clearing, then advanced driving, and lots of exposure to different weapons. Assault enemy positions or appear behind enemy lines to capture a high value target. Choose different locations all the time. Just mix it up. Might seem like no rhyme or reason, but the goal is repetition of many short courses which keep repeating, with variations. The result would be a vast, cycling exposure that will maximize broad experience *and* specialized skills. Also, keep it constructive and conversational – the goal should be exponential growth for each soldier"

In her spreadsheet, she had a column for notes. Nicole was furiously typing everything this man said. "Good, that's excellent. Again, we have to clear the locations but those are some really good ideas, from all of you." At that, Nicole looked up toward the aisle, and who should be walking toward the stage but the invisible man from the other day, wearing another outfit from his grey-on-beige line.

This man made his way on stage and shook Frank's hand, then Nicole's. "Good Afternoon everyone. My name is Juan, you may have seen me around." I remember that he had a deeper voice than I would have expected, and with very good voice control. "I have worked as a lawyer, I have worked for CNI, and now I work for the King. I will keep it brief, providing you answers to some of the questions I've heard. To cover the logistical question of locales first, you can use any location within reason, just provide me a list and it should be approved. Discussions of this war with the King mainly revolve around reinstalling the rule of law in America. Just as Spain has a good track record of using police and legal frameworks to uncover terrorist plots abroad, we believe the answer to America's problems are legal and political, and we believe Spain has insight to offer. I am sure the President agrees. I heard guerrilla warfare mentioned. By all means learn about how it's done, but do not do it. Training militias to fight for the government would merely create long-term problems in the guise of short-term solutions. I heard kidnapping mentioned. I would warn against using kidnapping per se – *arrests* are to be made where appropriate according to an agreed framework, which will be worked out soon. We've already been given legal authority to detain

American citizens on their territory upon arrival, but we need to work out issues of Spanish and International Humanitarian Law. War criminals are to be considered high value targets who should be taken alive whenever possible. If it is not possible, then alternatives can be used according to any legal means. To be clear, if you *can* take them in alive, you *must* take them in alive. This is the kind of war that makes one want vengeance, but wrath is not the law. Obviously, those who make war on you, will face war. It's a matter of drawing clear lines and sticking to them always. There shall be no torture. If you want to know what a prisoner knows, ask. Try to build rapport; get a prisoner to provide pieces to the puzzle that give you the answer, even without them providing the answer. Also, we are currently negotiating that *all* soldiers, US and NATO, use a signed loyalty oath to rebuild a nonviolent core to the population."

At this point Frank looked up again from whatever he was writing, took off his reading glasses, and asked, "You're thinking of asking for an Ironclad Oath? I think we looked into that a year ago and decided against it. There were issues with it after the first Civil War - created a lot of bad blood."

Juan answered, "That's because several issues were conflated in the loyalty oaths provided during the first American Civil War. First, Lincoln had to deal with the issue of readmission of states that had seceded, which none of yours have, and thus used the percentage of oaths signed in a state to quantify a point of admissibility back to the Union. We now know this is unnecessary. When a man knocks on your door and tells you he now owns your living room, you ignore him or call the police, not exhaust yourself with arguments and paperwork. Force is not authority, not even in wartime. If a state tries to secede, it has not actually seceded, since it has no right to secede. Those who will not concede to US legal authority, or international law, will find their arguments are null and their actions are sanctioned. Second, there was a faction who desired a punitive angle to those loyalty oaths, which was designed to prevent or limit political participation by former Confederates, and Lincoln feared being too hard on the South, then possibly losing the next election. There should be no punishment without a crime having been committed. In such situations as these, people can be coerced into taking illegal action in order to avoid a worse fate. A loyalty oath offers a choice, and protection. This brings me to the third and most critical point, which is the psychological value of getting signed loyalty oaths. Once signed, a person has chosen a side, and signed their name that they will not aid, counsel, encourage, or engage in hostility against the US. This can be done digitally to include fingerprint and facial recognition software. This can feed a vast intelligence network, working with any tips or advice provided by citizens. Lastly, those who commit war crimes, loyalty oath or not, shall be arrested and tried. Those who continue to make war shall be met with the doctrine of Total Warfare, within the bounds of international law. Our understanding is that reconstruction after the first Civil War was incomplete, which led to the Ku Klux Clan, Jim Crow, insurrectionists. Going back to sleep never works. Never. Do the right thing at the right time, for the right reasons. We believe that the only way is to absolutely crush all armed resistance, but lawfully, while rebuilding, and providing hope and trust under a better system. In this situation, a halfway victory would be a defeat. That is all!

He called out in a booming voice, ¡Viva España!

We fiercely called back in unison: *¡Viva!*

¡Viva el Rey!

¡Viva!

With that Juan briskly left the stage and walked into the dark at the back of the auditorium. Frank looked exasperated, but said he'd follow up on the loyalty oath conversation and provide direction later. The remainder of the question and answer session was also mainly about unresolved issues that Frank promised to follow up on. So we all left the auditorium with a good sense of the shape our training would probably take, and focused on victory.

Chapter 6

GOODBYES

We spent the rest of the first week being briefed on the Patriots, militias, and their tactics, as well as every other piece of information about the current state of affairs they could think of. Then near the end of the week, the big answers came. The planners had given us almost everything we wanted. We would still have about six months to train and travel, moving from place to place while cycling through trainings, usually more than once. As for FGNE, we would spend about one week in each different location: Ebro Valley in Aragon, Irati Forest in Navarra, the Ordesa Valley, the Riaño area, Redes Natural Park, and Valle de la Fuenfría, among many other traditional training areas like San Gregorio. American, French, German, British, Dutch, or Spanish Army, Marines, and Foreign Legion would often join us for a week or two. There were so many soldiers that would be shuffled in and out of various trainings; it must have been very complex to manage the logistics. Of course Nicole was our point of contact. Even though she wasn't directly in charge, she had the pull to get things altered or added when someone had a good idea. For instance, a few of us really pushed the idea of certain courses being shorter, unexpected, and more often, such as SERE or bush craft, and of course daily combatives. Everyone agreed that small unit tactics and close quarters' battle (CQB) should be trained frequently. We also asked for experts to cycle in on the combatives so we wouldn't know which style we'd be doing on any given day. Many asked for Brazilian Jiu-Jitsu, but also Tae-Kwon-Do, wrestling, boxing, Muay Thai, Shuai Jiao, MMA, and even a Spanish style. The Americans offered up advanced MCMAP, which is used by the Marines, the Israelis suggested Krav Maga, and the French suggested Savate. I suggested Tai Chi, combat applications. One of the most critical and consistent pieces of training was on spoken and written English. We also asked for training on knives and batons, since America would likely mean close quarters fighting and we were well aware of that. So we requested training on navaja, destreza, eskrima, silat and so on. Nicole took down everything requested and did her best to try to make it all happen, within the confines of what command agreed to, of course.

Luckily we had already received the newest graphene body armor, which provided incredible protection against most weapons, from armor piercing bullets to knives to lasers. We agreed on keeping but upgrading our rifles (HK416 variants), to include the newest networked optics. Our augmented reality night vision goggles were also upgraded again, so we needed training on using them, since it would all tie into the combat cloud and provide new capabilities.

The first weekend approached, and we were told in no uncertain terms to enjoy the time off, or take care of any necessary business, since we would be in the field almost constantly before being deployed overseas. We were also told in no uncertain terms what to say and not say. No discussion of our movement, training, ships, or equipment. In order to maintain operational security we would all tell our families that we'd be on a training mission for several months. We left for Cartagena early Friday morning. Hugo crammed Ben Zarco, Miguel, Neva and I in his Ateca and we set out for Cartagena. I put the idea forward that we could take the A-7 and P-7 to see the coast, but everyone wanted to get to their family so we took the A-92.

The sky was brilliant blue and the weather warm after raining all day Wednesday and Thursday. I rode in the passenger seat and the mood was excellent. Hugo even let us all take turns playing whatever music we liked. I had nothing against Sebastián, but I know if he had been with us he would have tried to make us listen to a dour podcast. We would have shouted him down! As we should. Neva picked out some really good American music, which made sense, so we all joined in the game of trying to find the best songs. We briefly stopped to eat but before we knew it we had arrived in Cartagena. A trip of several hours had gone by in a blink.

Our families had traveled to meet us there, some by plane or car, while some lived in town. My parents and Hugo's lived close, but all of us soldiers lived on base so it was the natural place for some of us to converge. Many others took flights to see their families. We had made arrangements to take over a restaurant for the night, so we could all get together one last time. My parents greeted me with hugs and kisses, as did everyone's. We made our introductions and re-acquaintances, everyone so happy. The warm air felt gorgeous that night. There was tapas and good conversation, and after watching the sun set over the mountains, we moved inside the restaurant. We made sure that in addition to all the other food on offer, we'd have some marinera and for our cocktail - reparo, oh, so much reparo. If I received a dollar for every "¡Salud!", I could have gone back to Belgium for free. Hugo did order one old-fashioned because, he quietly told us, that's what he would have ordered "while we were over there" but couldn't. Miguel poked a little fun at that but said something inadvertently accurate. He said Hugo always seemed like he might be from somewhere else. I agree with that observation.

Without detailing too much about our personal lives, we were all glad to be able to embrace, kiss, and just be near the ones we loved. Each of us spent time with each other's family in conversation. Miguel's parents, sisters, aunts, and cousins all made it, since they were local. Ben got to see his parents and sister. It was good to see

Neva's mother again, she will always be like an aunt to me. Hugo's father made us laugh with his stories and sharp wit. The night went on like that and we were all together for several lovely hours.

The sky was probably glittering with stars, but I couldn't see them due to all the city lights. The only solution might have been a dangerous and drunken scramble up the rocks to one of the old castles, the kind of ridiculousness of youth that always ends by collapsing in giddy laughter. Not anymore, of course.

When the hour finally arrived that the children were sleepy and everyone was satisfied, we all said our goodbyes among some tears and many hugs. I may not be the most social person, but I would not have left one minute early that night. I said my goodbyes too, and got into the back of my parent's Dacia Logan. I remembered the car they had when I was younger, before the accident.

Looking over at the empty seat beside me I wished my younger brother was still alive. Max was so much younger than me but still, I felt guilty for never spending enough time with him when I had the chance. I felt guilty because I was the driver. Right after the accident, that's when I joined the Marines. From then on I was responsible, dependable; I met my obligations head on, and excelled. I turned to look out the window at the receding restaurant closing down as we pulled out to drive home, and then facing front, broke the silence to tell my parents that I love them.

Chapter 7

DUEL

After what we treated like our last weekend, we all made our way to Algameca early Monday morning. Hugo lived close so he picked me up in the early morning before first light. As I got in, he handed me a coffee.

I asked, "Where did you get coffee this early? I didn't think anything was open."

"I know a guy."

"You know a guy who gets up early just to sell you coffee?"

"I do. Remember that place with the Mexican owner? Well I did him a big favor one time. So, you're welcome."

I took a sip. "Oh, this is really fucking good. Yeah, I remember that guy." I saw some pastries in a box too. "Oh, conchas!", I said, digging in.

Hugo laughed. "Hey, make sure we save some of those for the others."

We arrived on base in a very good mood, and ready to get to work. Regarding the intense training we were about to endure, when I didn't feel like sharing details in conversation later on, I would just say, "have you ever seen the training sequences in a kung-fu movie? Ok, imagine that but with modern weapons systems, and for six months, but no montage". The experience, in my opinion, was very useful and so I will not skip it here.

Further briefings, training, and most of all, a lively rumor mill, took up the first week back at base. The briefings were more blunt in that week, since it was our own officers and intelligence community speaking. We heard that cities like New York and Baltimore were attacked from within and without by small enemy action. Cities all faced hardship from local militias, hunger, disease, and disorder but some, like Washington D.C., Atlanta, and Miami, suffered all that and were savaged by larger militias, which sometimes also fought each other for control. Gangs filled in the gaps and unaffiliated criminals and grifters filled whatever space was left. It left the average citizen (who didn't want any part of this chaos) completely at a loss. The average family in the worst areas sometimes had children pressed into service by some gang or militia, or lost them in some pointless crime. What businesses still operated under the protection of the US military in the occupied zones faced constant attack, with employees and their families considered fair game. People did their best to help each other and many more would have died if not for the kindness and generosity of the common man. Still, all were left scarred, each in their own way.

The new US methods were hard-nosed but morally sound. The primary weapon in the new arsenal was essentially food diplomacy. Due to geographic advantages, safety, wealth, and especially food abundance, the decision was made for the US government to temporarily relocate to California. California was used both as a kind of giant aircraft carrier and fortress. Many troops who remained loyal along with military assets such as huge numbers of aircraft, main battle tanks, armored vehicles, artillery pieces and ships were all relocated there. Much needed food and supplies were then delivered to most large cities across the country by airdrops. The crates were all labeled with US flags stamped on top that said made in America. One could not help but notice that most of the items in each crate were labeled: "Product of California". Each crate had various foodstuffs. For instance they might contain staples like dried meat and cheese, cereal, flour, rice, and beans, but also dried fruits and nuts, including pistachios, almonds, and walnuts. Some candy or chocolate was often included. It's the small things that can sometimes boost morale the most, and they understood this. Each flight must have cost thirty or forty thousand dollars, so I can only imagine the bill for that effort. We were told that one of the main goals was to maintain and expand shipping options again, both rail and road. First, we'd have to defeat the enemy.

After the brief period back at base, we left for the Ebro Valley, which is in Aragon. We trained for more than a month there, learning not only small group action, but much larger scale operations. The terrain was difficult, with fields broken by tree-covered hills, the wide Ebro river, and mountains rising everywhere, some round and rolling, but many jagged and steep. We would break into blue team and red team, changing team members every three days or so. These were large-scale exercises involving air and land, sometimes small boat operations. Most of those coalition exercises were practiced with high-tech command and control, but some cycles we practiced low-tech solutions combined with modern best practices. For instance, runners on bicycle or foot transmitted some messages, which prevents any possibility of electronic interception. We practiced ways of protecting logistics and resupply such as food, water, and ammunition. The first month was very difficult on all of us. I think command just wanted to make sure we were all on the same page and could operate well together. Although I was in a Special Forces unit, so were many of the soldiers from other countries. We were all competitive, so breaking us up got everyone working together. It also gave me plenty of opportunity to practice my English. The terrain became the true enemy, so quick reaction groups often helped to get Special Forces behind enemy lines by using helicopters. There was one fatal incident where an American helicopter pilot was killed in a crash, with several injured. I was far away when it happened but I saw the smoke from a hill. These things happen of course, but it reminded us that they would happen more often in America. For some this added a bit of fear, and for others a bit of steel.

After a couple of weeks, these larger exercises gave way to a different pattern. We woke up early, practiced combatives of various kinds, small unit tactics and so on. I remember it was during this phase that we were introduced to destreza, or Spanish fencing. Destreza means dexterity, and I think that's why they agreed to teach it as one of the combatives. Hugo and I, along with my whole team, took to freeform fencing on time off with sticks and other things we'd find lying around. It greatly improves hand-eye coordination, speed, and agility. We got to be fairly skilled. The teacher, José, was an intense man and an excellent swordsman who would never let us win on the occasions we tried him. He was excellent at explaining his system to us though, and would answer questions in a most straightforward way. The challenge was that, when he wanted, we could not touch him. Granted, most of us were not fencers, but even those who were did not fare much better. When it was my turn I would try my best, but it can wear at your confidence to lose so badly and so often. He was always helpful though, and would explain what you did wrong; what he saw you thinking.

There is one story I'll relate from a kendo class that we also took. The teacher was named Kaito, who was also an excellent teacher and swordsman. Kaito's teaching style was different from José's, and was based more on mastery by practice. Anyway, one day we had just paired up to practice with shinai, which are the bamboo swords used in kendo. Thinking he was teaching us that day, José stepped into the room. There had been a mistake in scheduling. Kaito greeted him and they talked briefly. As José was leaving we all yelled and goaded them to spar with each other. They seemed bemused, but agreed to face off with shinai. Kaito had his sword raised above his head with both hands. José took a small step back with his left foot, right hand holding his sword pointed to the ground in front of his right leg. Other than the intensity of their eyes, neither seemed to move for half a minute, which stretched out like eternity. Finally, both of their feet seemed to slide forward at the same time, and they bowed to each other. We all booed! It was funny because we saw what was happening, but not how each of them knew what was happening. With that, José left and class continued. Afterward, we all asked Kaito about the match that didn't seem to materialize.

Miguel asked, "Why did you let the match end in a draw?"

Kaito smiled and said, "It wasn't a draw."

I asked, "Well, then who would have won?"

Neva suggested that Kaito would have won, but Hugo calmly disagreed.

"No, José would have won", he said with certainty.

Kaito said, "Excellent! And how do you know this?"

Hugo replied, "I don't know, but somehow I could see it in his eyes."

Kaito explained to us, "He would never have advanced, and if I had attacked he would have had me. I could see it. This is the greatest lesson you have learned today. Know yourself and know the opponent."

We thanked him and started out for the firing range. Neva said, "Damn it, I wanted Kaito to avenge me. That José needs a comeuppance."

I laughed and touched her arm, "You should never ask an acquaintance to avenge you. That's a lot of pressure on someone you barely know. Instead, say '*Try* to avenge me.'" I'll always remember my experiences in training, even though my eye-reading skills will never be top tier.

The teams continued to train for six months in various locations: the Irati Forest in Navarra, the Ordesa Valley, the Riaño area, Redes Park in the Cantabrian mountains, and Valle de la Fuenfría. We compared different training with other special forces – small unit and special tactics, solo survival, unconventional warfare, assault, demolition, hostage rescue, bushcraft, navigation, tracking, note-taking, SERE (survival, evasion, resistance and escape), parkour, martial arts, weapons, American language and culture, working with robots and automated vehicles, medical care, and more. We also received and trained on our new night-vision goggles with augmented reality, all networked by our combat cloud. This allowed the company to find new use cases through our exercises.

The last month of our training, we went through a Robin Sage-type exercise in Asturias along with our NATO allies. This was an excellent experience and I wish it was offered to all soldiers. Dave, Noah, and Ben (all green berets) stayed on during the entire exercise, consulting with leadership. As I mentioned before, we knew them as "the beards". Our teams were left in the Sierras de Cazorla natural park, a forested area with a large lake and rivers at the feet of many hills and mountains. The pine forest seemed endless, and many soldiers of the American Army were there to lend a more accurate feel to the exercise. Some were in uniform of course, but many others were in plain clothes, playing the part of friendlies, refugees, militiamen, sympathizers, as well as those who remained silent and neutral. Other than the beards, we didn't know who was who at the outset.

The basic premise of this large exercise was to train unconventional warfare mixed into the context of a conventional war. The Second American Civil War was much like the Spanish Civil War: brother against brother, interference by foreign powers, resentment and savagery. The exercise environment was created with all of this in mind. Should the Patriots take over entire sections of the United States, or should individual States secede, then simultaneous special operations, guerrilla action, and conventional warfare would overwhelm the enemy. There was a very realistic quality to the planning and the participants were hard to read. Instead of training indigenous guerrilla forces, which the Americans did not want, we would seek intelligence from the locals. In this way, we could benefit from what they saw, but not put them in danger. American guerrilla forces were dissuaded by their government. They would probably only have a one-to-one kill ratio, and the retaliation that would inevitably come was not worth it for them or the country.

Without describing all of the scenarios, we were training to solve ambiguous problems in a decentralized environment. The chaotic situations were designed to prevent us from getting direction from leadership. We had to devise solutions ourselves, and navigate the consequences. The reality on the ground in America was messy, so the training envisioned every flavor of mess. Kidnappings, terrorism, revenge killing, lawlessness, power outages, on top of floods, storms, and fires. Small villages had been created, where we would try to determine what to do. Every day was an unexpected problem we needed to solve. For example, we were imprisoned at one point, but Hugo escaped, then came back for us. Several of us escaped thanks to him, but there were not enough of us to get everyone out, which we tried. In most areas, the population of this mock country held a certain number of core enemy surrounded by sympathizers, then many neutral parties trying to avoid conflict, and, finally, a group who wanted to return authority back to the government of the USA. Each village had a different mix of these groups, and it was a mess. We had to develop relationships, locate the enemy, then plan and execute action accordingly. I credit this exercise with giving us a realistic glimpse into just how uncertain and brutal things would get. Still, the map is not the territory.

Chapter 8

DELMARVA

After training, most of us stayed focused on the tasks at hand. Some followed the news, listening for clues. Because of this everyone knew what was coming, but some fooled themselves into thinking they knew exactly when, and how. The plan, we heard, was to try to get all our troops into Joint Force Command Norfolk, but this war was never straightforward, as we'd see for ourselves. We were told that the invasion would take place in mid-to late May, but it was the beginning of a cold and overcast April 14th when the ships left. The sight of thousands of troops boarding those grey ships on a grey morning was more banal than I would have thought. I watched them leave, slowly receding from view until they had gone beyond the horizon. The NEX and commissary shelves were nearly empty but I spent some time getting last minute essentials. My team was gathered later that morning with the others and briefed. The destination was revealed to be the large peninsula they call "Delmarva" (because Delaware, Maryland and Virginia all make up part of that territory). Although we were not told about it, there was an intelligence operation to sow doubt about where we might land. Later I heard that Florida and South Carolina were insinuated to be landing zones, but I was not privy to any of that at the time. Delmarva was a good choice because it was nearly an island, like Spain, and could therefore be used to project power along the eastern seaboard.

When it was time to go, it turned out that the special forces would be sent by a more comfortable ride than the Navy could have provided. America was kind enough to fly us into New York City by way of the Civil Reserve Air Fleet. From New York City, where many of the C-5M Super Galaxies, C-17s, and A400M Atlases had been staged, we would fly down and jump into Dover Air Force Base. The thinking must have been to hide in plain sight. We arrived at night, with troops from several countries joining US counterparts, and were shuttled from commercial planes over to military planes. Some US soldiers had joined us all the way from their European post, such as US Navy SEALs with NSWU-10 from Rota. With the ongoing war and how busy JFK and LaGuardia are, I don't think too many noticed. It was also very late, actually the early morning of the 15th. We did not enter the airport, as we didn't want to telegraph our movement, but it was The City, so there were eyes everywhere. We got into lines and walked up the waiting ramps, into the dark, cavernous interiors of the transports, and sat down. All of us were crammed together, loaded with our gear, sitting along four columns running nearly the length of the plane, each line looking over at the other. The flight was short, and I was focused and ready. There would be no HALO jump that night. When it was time, I heard "outboard stand up", then hooked up for a static line jump. We checked our equipment. The doors were pulled upward on each side to reveal the darkness, and the light was still red. We heard the commands; the light went yellow. Then came the familiar hand gesture and I heard the countdown: four, three, two, one, green light! We jumped one after another, in quick succession, from the interior of the plane to the cold dark of the night. In the day, I might have glanced back to see the parachutes of those behind me opening – looking first like umbilical cords, then jellyfish. That night was quite dark, with clouds mostly covering the stars. I could see that this land was exceptionally flat. The planes were already turning back to continue their mission, bringing more soldiers in. A gentle landing and a short walk over to our teams, and we were in America.

Due to occasional attacks and redeployment elsewhere, Dover's personnel had gone from about 6000 down to 2000. Some of that redeployment of US troops was around Delmarva to disrupt any local enemy surveillance or small group action. We got dropped with about 600 paratroopers on the first night, plus vehicles, anti-tank weapons, and so on. Attack helicopters provided protection, but not one shot was fired. The next night brought in many more soldiers and a decent number of necessary vehicles. In one aspect it got easier in the days following since there was no enemy activity, so planes were landing to offload. The vast majority of our troops and vehicles, such as Leopards, Dragons, VAMTACs, helicopters, drones, and transports, would come in later by sea. Being on one of the initial teams on the ground, I felt lucky to have at least a few days to get acclimated. The US troops we talked to at Dover mostly verified everything we were briefed about. Our teams had been dropped a week prior to the NATO armada arriving so, in truth, we were all waiting tensely and keeping busy. Engineering and construction of new facilities was impressive. The number of troops on Delmarva would soon exceed 150,000 and it couldn't come fast enough.

Even though thousands of additional troops were deployed without incident in the next few days, we knew this could be the calm before the storm. To be safe, we made sure to break part of our force into many small groups in the first week, placed in defensive positions. We also tried to harden Dover as best we could. The Patriots clearly had good intelligence and must have been watching for us via local networks. We set up sensors and flew small reconnaissance drones over the area. After no enemy contact for the first few days, the Patriots began a sudden push to take Norfolk.

Carlos had talked to the Americans at this time, and we had our orders. The kind of order a soldier waits for. I will not state our original expected destination, but FGNE teams were flown down in several helicopters, a trip so long they needed in-flight refueling. We were informed that the engagement at Norfolk was on a much larger scale than any previous attacks. The enemy had set up mobile artillery many kilometers from the base, causing a number of US casualties. Patriots were also inside the city, striking behind US lines. Hahn was trying to close in on Norfolk, but a day of heavy bombing kept his forces moving and unable to take the base. Counterattacks by US Special Forces dealt targeted damage to the enemy, keeping us in the fight. The NATO Armada was also closing in, and Hahn's luck was seemingly running out.

Chapter 9

ATLANTIC

As the Armada approached America, they were unaware of what the enemy had planned. The Patriots, having also infiltrated the US Navy, made sure they were all on duty at once to maximize their chances at Norfolk. They had already hazed those they distrusted, assigned their own people to certain ships, and maintained a very neutral and patriotic demeanor. The Patriots thus sent out what was effectively their own navy, such as littoral combat ships, patrol ships, and stolen civilian boats, to block the European Armada. Initially, our response would have been to smash through what was an inferior but still dangerous navy. Two US destroyers set out from Norfolk to protect the European Armada and attack the Patriots from another angle. The Patriot navy would have been daunting enough, but a destroyer was violently stolen several hours earlier that we were not informed about. The Zumwalt, which the Patriots had managed to storm by treachery and supplement with their own crew, was much more threatening to our ships. They had sailed it into open ocean, where the low radar cross-section and long standoff distance meant trouble. Tomahawk missiles, for instance, might be better for attacking land, but they were accurate and had a range of 1500 nautical miles. The Zumwalt had a lot of them, so the Armada was not safe.

Hahn's forces used the Zumwalt to fire missiles at Norfolk's ships from miles out at sea, while menacing our own armada with a saturation attack. Our ships took evasive action and applied electronic warfare systems to block and jam course correction by the missiles. The British and the French both returned fire with multiple anti-ship missiles. Since the British were closest, they dealt the final blow using their Carrier Air Wing. It appeared to have also been damaged by a French Exocet, but in any case the Zumwalt was finished. Most of the remaining Patriot ships in the first wave of any considerable size were spammed with various missiles from our allied armada and sunk. There had been several British and French casualties and minor damage, but no ships sunk. The Spanish ships, by chance, were positioned opposite the enemy upon engagement. All the same, our ships made good use of their Naval Strike Missiles.

One story I can pass along, as told to me by two separate British sailors, was of trying to save the American Patriots after the Zumwalt sunk. The sailors were stationed on a UK destroyer during the battle and saw everything first hand. Their destroyer had moved to pick up any surviving crew after the Zumwalt sank, making several announcements over the speakers. The Patriots refused to board, probably out of resistance, or perhaps feeling that their own ships would save them. A couple even impotently fired their pistols at the destroyer from the waves below. No one fired back. The British simply sailed away, slowly, blaring their national anthem at the traitors. One of the sailors who told me this story said, "it was fucking brilliant".

During this time the Patriots were attacking Norfolk by air to suppress and tie up US air power. A second order from a senior officer came through, sending four more destroyers to "respond" to Hahn's attacks, which charted their own courses once free. The last three of the four US destroyers simply sailed away, toward Washington, Baltimore and Philadelphia, to everyone's confusion. In response, the first ship to depart in that wave (which had stayed in communication with the Americans) received orders from another commander to attack the other three ships. The lead ship did indeed turn back, but then fired on the remaining destroyers still in port, causing severe damage. The other three destroyers joined in, firing several more missiles at the docked ships. Many of the destroyers in port were on fire, and bathed in dark smoke that choked the air. The thick plumes could be seen drifting with the wind for miles.

Meanwhile, Hahn had also used small attack boats and Patriot direct action units along the Chesapeake and Delaware Canal (and its bridges) to cut off Delmarva. Around quarter after noon, he ordered several missiles apiece fired into Washington, Baltimore, and Philadelphia causing serious damage to military targets. In Washington D.C., the Marine barracks and Joint Base Myer–Henderson Hall were both hit, along with Joint Base Andrews. Baltimore was struck directly, causing numerous civilian casualties downtown. The third ship had sailed up Delaware Bay, and then fired missiles into McGuire Air Force Base and a few Navy facilities, including the Naval Surface Warfare Center. NAVSEA and NAVAIR were struck, along with Surface Forces Logistics Coast Guard and Camp David.

Hahn sent demands for the immediate surrender of all three cities, and demanded that the President and Vice-President step down immediately. Almost as an afterthought, the Patriots fired missiles at Joint Expeditionary Base–Little Creek. The problem was, with all the commotion, nearly every ship had been put out to sea, and military personnel evacuated. The Navy SEALs, for instance, were based at JEB Little Creek, and could have gotten wiped out by a storm of missiles, if not for the Patriot's poor timing. Buildings can always be rebuilt, but the people mostly escaped. Even the damage to buildings and other assets at Little Creek was not as bad as it could have been. Too much of the enemy's focus was on threatening civilians. I suppose Hahn never thought that, when faced with an armed enemy and an unarmed civilian, you shoot the armed one? Terror only turns a population against you.

There were really only four options to deal with the destroyers stolen by the Patriots. Complicating this, the Americans originally wanted to save the ships of course. European submarines weren't close enough to act fast, and the Americans worried that scrambling nearby subs from Norfolk was a gamble, given that ships had already been taken. We could board the vessels by helicopters. That would be a bloody fight, since each ship was almost fully manned, and by zealots. We could have killed every last one of them, at a cost, but they would either fire all missiles at the cities, blow up the ships with us on them, or both. That method was not quick enough. The Patriots had already shown so much violence of action that a cautious approach would not have worked. The third option would be to bombard the ships with missiles. Each destroyer could do an excellent job of defending itself but would eventually be sunk. Not, however, before turning each city center into a fiery tomb. Skyscrapers and office buildings might be struck, collapsing with thousands of civilians inside, raining chunks of concrete, bodies, and steel down onto pedestrians below. This option we also rejected. Lastly, frogmen could sink the ships. With this choice, we agreed. This was what we trained for. The US President and his people would personally call and negotiate with General Hahn, while small teams of frogmen planted bombs on each ship. The timers would be synchronized to prevent any advance warning, and they'd all sink at once. That was the hope.

Carlos, as our commanding officer, chose Hugo to lead a team of four to actually sink the destroyer that attacked Philadelphia. Hugo, Miguel, Ben, and I would be passengers on a manned submersible that would allow us to approach and plant a mine. The Navy SEALs would sink the ship that had attacked Washington, D.C, and the UK's Special Boat Service would take the destroyer that had attacked Baltimore. France's Commando Hubert and SEAL teams both volunteered for the most difficult job of sinking the ship that had been directly attacking Norfolk. We agreed that the time could be set at 2:20 p.m. to minimize the amount of negotiation between the US President and General Hahn. A plan having been formed, simple as it was, we set out to destroy the destroyers.

The destroyer threatening Philadelphia was situated past Cape May. We set out in a very low flying helicopter, which got us within three miles by using land for cover. I spotted ghost forests in the distance, where saltwater had killed all the trees leaving an eerie landscape behind. The dark bay was cold at 14°C, and the helicopter lowered its back end gently into the water, partly submerging us. Once we were on the submersible, which also had a crew of two, the four of us passengers prepared over the next hour as we closed in. We knew there were several different teams trying to sink the other destroyers, while the US President was simultaneously negotiating with the Patriots. With so much going on above the surface (and below), we stayed serene and focused on the objective. The ship was also undermanned due to the takeover, so we hoped not to be spotted.

Our target was the Arleigh-Burke class destroyer "USS Hale". Without divulging much, we had some level of protection from ultrasound, but we were on the lookout for anything from remote-controlled underwater vehicles to trained dolphins. Once we reached our target, two large mines were placed near the bottom of the hull and the timers set. Then we retreated back to the agreed location, where the helicopter picked us back up. I'll admit that I secretly wanted to see the ship sink, but the helo was flying very low and the pilot was focused on staying alive. We heard the massive explosion but were already beyond line of sight. I won't lie, hearing that sound sent a surge of adrenaline through me. The pilot looked back and gave us the thumbs up, and we later heard that the mines had lifted the Hale out of the water, breaking its spine. Our team had completed the operation without losing anyone or getting captured.

The helo took a roundabout path toward Norfolk, approaching the dark clouds of smoke rising from ships and buildings. We were told to stay in a large brick building at the Norfolk Naval Station. Many of the Spanish troops I knew were there, and a portion of the third army came not long after. The EU fleet had offloaded unopposed once they reached Wilmington in Delmarva, Baltimore, Philadelphia, and also NAVSTA Newport in Rhode Island. Those ships could be repositioned later. The enemy had fallen dead silent, but there was much work ahead. The wrecked ships would need to be cleared and repaired. There were heavy losses of soldiers, contractors, and civilians throughout the area. The Americans would be solemn and busy in the coming weeks. Nonetheless, at least among our own, we knew what a victory we had helped to secure.

Chapter 10

WANDS

There was celebration everywhere that night, as if the entire war had been won. To celebrate I took advantage of hot water, soap, and some cocoa butter that Neva had brought. I was washing up and heard music, laughter, and shouting from outside. I threw on my clothes and let Neva in. I came out of the bathroom, just having taken a hot shower, to find everyone was starting some sort of crazy impromptu barracks party. There were lights being strung up and lots of food being brought in. Sadly there was no alcohol, since it was strictly prohibited for the duration of our service there, but everyone was in good spirits. I ate Chinese food that someone had ordered. Ben and Jesse were in the kitchen cooking, and it all smelled great. I swear people turn to hot food during war for comfort. When I cracked open my fortune cookie it read, "Love is on the horizon". I remember eating it with a private smile on my face.

Hugo was holding court on a couch in the middle of the room, telling stories, smoking and waving his hands around for emphasis. Our people were sitting all around him, laughing and talking, music blaring. As I made my way over, it was "Ndeleng Ndeleng" playing loudly, and everyone was smiling, chatting. Clearly Hugo was the DJ.

There was food and drink already spread around the edges of a wooden coffee table in the center of the room. I was just hanging back, taking it all in. He saw me with my towel still wrapped around my head and, smiling broadly, motioned to a nearby plush chair, calling out, "Alba! Just in time, come sit down. Look what I found. Someone left these here." With the music turned up, we had to raise our voices. A cigarette dangling from his mouth, he picked up a messy deck of tarot cards from the table and started shuffling intensely.

I laughed but protested, "I already got my fortune tonight, and you're going to try to tell me my future anyway, huh?"

"Alba, I've never known anyone who didn't want to know their future except you!"

I grunted but agreed to let him do my reading. "I didn't even know you could do tarot!"

"You know me, I'm a man of the world... and modest", he said as he smiled wryly, still shuffling. "I'll do a kind of Celtic cross."

Miguel looked at me, then back at the cards, furrowing his brows. "Hugo, I hope her reading isn't half as dark as mine. You know what mine was, Alba? That I would lose people I care about. I don't need to hear that shit, especially not over here." Then Miguel flicked a corn chip at Hugo who brushed it off with the back of his hand without looking.

The shuffling had stopped. Then Hugo looked up at me, "Ok, Alba. The first card represents you", he said pulling a card and looking at it before laying it down in the center of the table. He nodded a little in approval. It was a crowned woman in a blue and white robe sitting on a throne at the ocean's edge, looking at a large golden chalice. "This is the Queen of Cups. She is loving, intelligent, honest, pure of heart, and wise."

"All that, and modest?" I quipped.

Hugo smiled and looked at me from under his brows, "Alba, did you steal my joke?"

"You can't prove it" I shot back with a dismissive smile and a wave of my hand.

"Ok", he said, sitting back and drawing the next card. He held it up, looking at it before laying it sideways across the Queen of Cups. "This is your challenge; your obstacle: Death."

"Ok, so I die too? Bullshit, I'm with Miguel" I said, throwing a corn chip at Hugo.

Hugo put his hands up diplomatically, "The death card does not necessarily mean you die, it can mean that you or others will face death, or see death, or even just go through some other transformation. But let's be honest, we're in the middle of a war. It probably means there will be death all around us. This is the obstacle." Even with the music still blaring, I noticed at this point that everyone was listening.

"So…what it says"

"Yes Alba, what it says. Next are your influences; the *conscious* ones" Hugo went for the third card, which he placed above the first two to form the top of the cross. It was a woman floating in the sky holding a rod in each hand, encircled by a sort of wreath, with figures at each corner. "This is good – The World. It means success, voyage, wisdom, completeness, sharing what you've gained, the realization of great work, the fulfillment of cycles. Maybe it's all the philosophy you've been reading. The next card will be your *subconscious*, the root of some things." He pulled a card to make the bottom of the cross. A woman in a red dress, head down, was blindfolded and tied up, standing on marshy ground in front of a mountain, with swords impaled into the ground surrounding her. "This is the eight of swords."

"So I'm a prisoner of my subconscious?" I asked. "I'd rather focus on the World card."

"Well, not exactly, this is emotional or mental, but look – there is no one around. She can free herself at any time. She just needs to realize that she isn't obligated to remain stuck in place forever. She can be happy. Make sense? Next is your past."

I nodded, sort of understanding, but waved my hand on to the next one. The next card made the left side of the cross, and it was two children in a village with several golden goblets filled with flowers. The older child is handing one of the goblets to the younger.

"This is the Six of Cups", said Hugo. With this he watched my eyes, "It represents memories, youth, the happiness of the past, things and people that are gone now. Next is your future." He pulled out another card and made the right arm of the cross, completing it. This card was a high tower with lightning striking the top, flames coming from the windows, and two figures falling toward the ground.

"The Eleven of Septembers?" I asked darkly.

"Wow. Jesus, Alba" Hugo said, pulling his hand down across his forehead and eyes. "No, this is The Tower. This represents a moment – a crisis, or a turning point. It is a calamity, but one that you must confront. That's how you move forward. Ok, now I have to draw four more cards."

"Oh god damn, if you haven't killed me off yet..." I joked.

"A little trust", he replied. He lined up the four cards in a column off to the right side of the cross. "I'll read these bottom to top. The bottom of the column is your attitude."

"*My* attitude?...*You're* an attitude" I joked again.

Hugo laughed and said, "¡Anda! Ok, your attitude is The Hermit.

"Let me guess, he's looking for wisdom."

"No, he's trying to share it – look at his lantern, there is a star in there. He already attained wisdom; he's trying to shine a light for others. Moving up, the next card is your environment, which is the seven of swords. You can see this guy stealing five of these swords from a military encampment. Impulsive, greedy, duplicitous, hidden dishonor. Above that is your hopes and fears - The Hanged Man. Look at his face - he represents contemplation, suspending life; he's not moving in one direction or another until he figures it out. Just don't wait forever to start living Alba. Ok, at the top of the column is your outcome. The outcome of all of this is the nine of wands."

"¡Buaah! He's got a little towel wrapped around his head, just like me" I said playfully.

"Ok, first off, that's a bandage" he said.

I picked up the card. "You're right. And he doesn't look happy." It was a wary and troubled man in a red tunic, hair tousled, bandage wrapped around his head, tightly holding a staff with both hands. There were nine other wands driven into the ground behind him. Unlike the eight of swords, these staffs seemed to have been claimed from his defeated enemies. "Wait, counting the nine staffs behind him plus the one he's holding, there are ten."

Hugo, looked through the deck for a card, "Yeah. Take a look at the ten of wands: in that one he's carrying all the wands back to the village."

"Why would he do that?" I asked.

"Well, it seems to be the oppression of victory; the weight of things done" Hugo explained.

"It seems to be PTSD. If he defeated his enemies in the Nine of Wands, the mission is over. Drop the weight. His fight is done. To quote the Tao Te Ching: 'When the work is done, it is forgotten. That's why it lasts forever'."

"Well Alba, since you see it beforehand, maybe it will be easy for you to set the weight down. It's easier to know a thing than to feel a thing." There was something in the way he said it that made me feel like I might have let *him* down. Not that he disagreed with me, but that even though I understood, I didn't understand both sides *in my bones*. I had seen combat, but hadn't gathered ten staffs, and I certainly wasn't carrying them all. I couldn't fathom why it should be so hard to set them down. He reached over and gently took the card back, placing the neat deck back on the table.

I just nodded apologetically and thanked him for the reading. "Do you want some more food? Jessenia made some great shrimp…"

"Thanks Alba, I'm good. I'm just going to go outside to get some air for a minute."

"Ok" was all I could say.

Taking his phone with him, someone else had to pick up as DJ so it was back to top ten hits from home. I took the towel off my head and threw on my jacket to follow Hugo downstairs. As I stepped out into the night the air felt chilly, probably because my hair was still wet. Hugo was leaning against a brick wall smoking a cigarette and looked up, a little surprised to see me. His phone was sitting next to him on the wall, still playing at a low volume. I walked over and leaned on the wall next to him.

"Hey. I just want to say sorry. Whatever you've seen, whatever you've been through, I don't want you to think I'm judging you."

Hugo said "I don't. I *have* seen things. But I was thinking about you. I worry that someday you'll be standing where I am now, but alone. As much as you think you can let everything go easily…I don't know if it will work out that way. We all go through things, but it's never good to be too closed off. When those times come, you just have to try to make peace with your life, and don't be afraid to reach out to people. You know?"

"I'm a soldier, just like you. This is war. No one needs to worry about me" I said defensively. I looked toward the city, dim buildings backed by a gauzy sunset undercutting a sky of ominous clouds. Softening I added, "Sometimes I feel like…if I open the door, even a little, life will toss in a hand grenade." I sighed. "Listen…if it ever reaches that point, if I feel like I need to lean on someone…I will. Promise."

Hugo exhaled, "That's good, I'm glad to hear it."

A sadder song had come on so I leaned over to see. It was called "Thioro Baye Samba", by Star Band de Dakar. "Why is this guy so bummed out?"

He took a drag from his cigarette, looked up at me and smirked, "He's got a huge crush on this beautiful girl."

"Yeah?"

"Yeah, he's got it bad. But she acts aloof. She won't marry any of the neighborhood guys because their families are lower class, including the singer." He took another drag from his cigarette. "So he's talking to himself, trying to figure out why she acts that way. He knows she won't budge, not even if he came into money and her mom approved. He imagines secretly going by her father's house at night and seeing him eating the supper of a poor man. Then it all makes sense. He realizes that she must be from a lower class family too, and she's just avoiding marrying a man who came from the same hard places. So the sadness comes not only from the girl avoiding him, but seeing how the world helped shape that."

Watching his eyes I reached over, gently took the cigarette from him, and after taking a slow drag off it, exhaled. "I would tell him...don't give up on her". My lips curled up a little as I handed his cigarette back and exhaled.

Before Hugo could answer, Sebastián spilled out the door, looking embarrassed. He seemed like he was hoping he would be alone, and looked a little off. Hugo greeted him, but Sebastián only said, "Hey, I just came down for a smoke too. They're looking for you guys upstairs." With that he lit up a cigarette, perhaps to keep himself silent. I'm not sure if he was trying to get rid of us, or if everyone genuinely noticed Hugo and I were gone for a little while together.

Hugo nodded and turned to head back in, dropping his cigarette into a plastic smoker's receptacle. I teased him about not flicking it onto the ground while in the middle of a war zone. He said, "That's why things go to shit though. The world needs more janitors, more garbage men, more builders. Soldiers are only around to make it safe. I want to see them rebuilding, even better than before. I'll know we've made a difference when I see cranes lining the streets." We ducked past Sebastián, opening the door as we talked. Entering the vestibule my eye caught a single blond hair hanging from Hugo's right sleeve. As he started up the stairs I timed my grab perfectly, removing it. When we got back to the party, no one mentioned anything. Not that we did anything wrong anyway. Still, I felt relief.

Chapter 11

ART

The quiet had been too good to last. A week after the conflict at Norfolk ended, several cities, including Richmond, had come under a concerted invasion by Patriot forces backed by local militias. Some smaller towns and cities did fall to the enemy, but Richmond was by far the largest to do so. I'm told they had planned to counterattack Washington, D.C., which is only 100 miles distance, had they been able to consolidate power in the area. This was a well coordinated campaign by the Patriots to maintain their initiative. It turned out that a large number of sympathizers and their families had fled before midnight, and the invasion began at 0200. There was excellent coordination of the attacks, which included some air power. I know several drones were shot down over Richmond, as well as an AC-130, but not before it had decimated some of the local military and police assets. Obviously there were civilian casualties as well. The Patriots never cared much about losing aircraft, because they were invariably stolen and wouldn't last forever on the ground. Every helicopter or jet the Patriots stole could be turned against America and, even if destroyed, that meant one less asset for Uncle Sam.

I won't attempt to fully recount the siege, since we had not yet arrived to witness it ourselves.

Between artillery and bombs, I do know that extensive damage had already been done to the city before we saw it. Buildings lay in ruin, electricity cut out, water stopped, and civilians fled in every direction. Traffic snarled, with bullet riddled cars left lining the streets. The Patriots sent their Special Forces groups sweeping in to take out the city's government and those police who remained loyal. I felt bad for the police, who did their best against long odds, I'm sure.

Patriots took control of the bridges over the James River, along with colleges, city hall, and the airport. This cut off many important roads, like the I-95. Tanks and APCs took up positions and dug in. Helicopter gunships buzzed by in waves, occasionally striking at targets. I talked to some of the civilians after the battle. They told me about going to high ground or rooftops in the first surreal moments, watching huge fireballs rising from the street and ducking when shock waves shattered glass. In fact, their city had fallen under a siege for the third time. Burned by Benedict Arnold, then again by Grant, and now by Hahn. The irony was probably not lost on the citizens in Richmond.

We were all put on alert, briefed, and prepared to free Richmond. UK and French forces would be greater in number than Spanish forces during the battle for the city, but we intended to do our part. A large number of the citizens who were not tipped off by the Patriots to flee on the first night were trapped inside the city, and not permitted to leave. Checkpoints were manned by militia at every important intersection. Any remaining citizens were essentially hostages. All the same, most eventually managed to slip out by various means. Those who were caught, or fought back, were shot. The Americans immediately tried to negotiate for release of the residents on humanitarian grounds, but the enemy consolidated their control around both Richmond and Petersburg, which is a smaller city just to the south. The orders came down that we would retake Richmond. This was to be an overwhelming force of around 15,000 NATO troops, with about 10,000 being Americans. The majority of those Americans were marines, joined by roughly 2500 Spanish and 2500 British. The Americans, along with a large French and German contingent, would be ready to assault Petersburg, the most likely place the fleeing enemy would try to regroup. There were several thousand of the enemy at most, but they had the means to defend themselves and their newly acquired territory. The Patriots also seemed to have no end to their surprises.

Initially, NATO drones did reconnaissance over the city, mapping troop locations and gathering proof of war crimes. Once there was a good idea of the basic defenses put in place by the enemy, multiple sorties dropped precision strikes each night to minimize the chance of civilian casualties and keep the Patriots on the defense. Those positions where the enemy had dug in too well had to be left for ground forces. Enemy armor were sometimes parked near or under major buildings for instance. The James Monroe building, the tallest in the city, was filled with militia and Patriot snipers. All of this had been discussed with the Americans beforehand, and there were no good options. We were to try to preserve the city as best we could, which meant that we could not put air superiority to its greatest use. The only viable option, we were told, was to clear everything, house by house, office by office. We had superiority in numbers, equipment, communications, logistics, and everything else, but they were determined to hold their ground or die. Each day we watched them training in the city: target practice, rebuilding defenses, knocking mouse-holes in the walls for snipers. Each night we'd target them with precision munitions and drones to keep them off balance. Loud and horrific sounds, like crying babies that morphed into demonic shrieking, were played at deafening volume to prevent sleep. Ultrasound whispered dreadful thoughts. Our planners gamed out each possibility, knowing that this wouldn't be clean. Urban warfare always favors the defender.

Every day we practiced clearing buildings and destroying fortified positions until everyone moved clean and in unison. We also brushed up on shoot / no-shoot drills for every possible situation, which was interesting. For the solo drills, there would be a bag on our head that was pulled off and, each time, there was a different scenario in front of us. Sometimes it might be a woman with a child, or a gunman, or someone asking directions. We also studied the territory. Maps and sand-tables attracted soldiers like gazelles around a watering hole. We made forays into certain neighborhoods for reconnaissance at night. It was clear that if we waited too long, the Patriots would have such a stranglehold on the city that it would be difficult to take even partially intact. A balance was struck between acting swiftly to save the people who remained in Richmond, and being prepared. The Americans set the D-day and H-hour to start taking the city back.

When the hour came, it happened in this way. The Americans commenced a simultaneous missile attack in an attempt to destroy all the enemy artillery, mortar teams and missile launchers they could find in the city. Although mechanized divisions accompanied us throughout the operation to free Richmond, most of the fighting would need to be done by marines. Then the armies would move in to hold the city. Americans, Canadians, British, French, and Spanish groups all encircled the enemy north and east of the James river. We did not want to encircle the Patriots from the South as well, which would have destroyed the city and its people in the process. As Sun Tzu said, when you surround your enemies, leave an opening. The plan was to drive the enemy out of downtown Richmond using attacks from the north and east, but leaving enough space to allow a retreat south across the James using bridges. For this reason, we didn't want the bridges along the James River blown, so we'd need to allow the enemy to feel it was not in their interest to do so until it was too late. Beyond the James river, and south of the city, we would have a freer hand to destroy the enemy.

A number of important sites had to be taken back over the first week. The high ground throughout Richmond was critical, but it was held by Patriot forces and militia. Artillery and mortar fire could rain down on our coalition forces if they were not cleared. The US Marines began to take that ground back, one hill at a time, which lead to a series of cemetery battles. Cemeteries seemed to occupy much of the high ground in the city and the joke was, if you were killed there fighting, they wouldn't even have to move you. There were tough and bloody fights at Union hill, Hollywood cemetery, all over Shockoe Hill, and Church Hill. Attack helicopters were very helpful in some of those battles, even though three birds were lost, along with their crew. The Patriots had secured enough man portable missiles to inflict those casualties, but the marines would not be stopped.

Despite several dead and wounded the marines pushed forward relentlessly both day and night, so that, within the first three days, most of the high ground was held by the Yankees. Dozens of Patriot tactical trucks and APCs were left smoldering until each area was deemed clear. Plumes of smoke rose from the hills as proof of their victory, until a summer rain doused the burning vehicles.

The Americans struck everywhere. The Navy SEALs were tasked with taking back the State Capital Complex and Executive Mansion. I'm not sure if that's because Uncle Sam didn't trust us as foreign troops to take those sites but, speaking only for the Spanish, we would not have used that opportunity as a pretense to gather information. Most information can be gathered through open sources and, anyway, it would be a breach of trust. The SEAL teams went on a night raid, roping in to capture the State Capital. Sniper teams took up positions on the captured high ground surrounding the site. The marines pushed through each section of the residential area, clearing everything house by house.

We continued to stay ready in those first few days, before finally getting a mission. The Virginia Museum of Fine Arts had been occupied by the Patriots as a sort of high-art hostage situation. During the final missions brief we were tasked with raiding the museum at night, which would be coordinated with a power outage. The utility workers had been left unharmed, although the Patriots had raided their offices and substations in an attempt to coerce control of the electric grid. The utility asked only to continue operating, and thus they were generally left alone. The Americans had managed to devise a plan with the utility, where their operators would cut power to the museum directly from the substation. This would impact only the museum without alerting other locations.

At 0300 hours, the power to the museum was cut, just as we arrived to rope in from helicopters. Dressed all in black, we were armed with suppressed P90s to prevent excess damage to the facility. 32 team members participated in all. There were four teams and four ways in: the Boulevard entrance, the Group entrance, the Main entrance, and the Sculpture Garden entrance which we'd take. Since the power had been cut, we wanted to move through quickly in case they had night vision. We did hear some yelling, but no flashlights came on, which was an ominous sign.

We saw two sentries trying to hide from view using the hardscape, so we marked them and took them out. We waited to see if there was any reaction, but the commotion was inside. As each team slowly closed in on the entrances, a sniper tried to take us out. I heard the crack of the bullet loudly echo across the lawn. We took cover and started laying down suppressing fire. I saw Neva creep off to the side; she had the shot. Several shots rang out, and the sniper rolled away from his gun. She fired three more times, until he stopped writhing.

The gunfire attracted the Patriots inside the museum, and they trained their fire on us. AR-15s were firing at the hardscape we used for cover, but when they opened up with a .50 cal, the walls began to chip and crumble. Over the radio, the three other teams announced entry and started clearing the building. Little pieces of the wall flew past, some scraping my cheek as bullets struck. We kept firing and moving positions to avoid them punching big holes through the wall. Finally, we heard gunfire and confusion as our team mates arrived from behind the enemy. We kept our heads down as they cleared out the Patriots who had us pinned just moments before. Once our soldiers shouted out the all clear, we went down to the entrance.

Hugo went up to Sanz, who was a soldier on one of the other teams. "We thought we were in trouble for a minute!"

"You know, there were only a couple of people guarding our entrance, so we should thank you fuckers for making all that noise! I think everyone in the building decided to take a shot at you" said Sanz.

"Well, it's the least we could do. I'm glad you showed up when you did though", Hugo replied.

Sanz tapped Hugo lightly on the chest, "Come see this". We followed him in, not know what we'd find.

Stepping over the bodies of the enemy as we walked, I asked, "What is it Sanz? I see them, but I'm not sure what I'm looking for."

"Look up."

I lifted my flashlight. "Oh shit", I said slowly. In the halls, small metal hooks and paper markers remained at intervals where paintings once hung. Looking down the hall, not one painting remained.

"It's like this in all the other sections, nothing."

"Have you covered the whole building? Maybe they're just hidden somewhere", Hugo asked.

"We're clearing every room, but knock yourselves out."

So we searched all four levels. We looked in every room and closet, every bathroom, and behind everything that wasn't bolted to the wall. By the way, I just wanted to put on record that the Patriots had made a mess of the place while living there. There was an awful smell and they left chicken bones on the tables. It was disgusting. We looked through the museum for so long that someone called in the all clear, and the utility workers cut the lights back on from the substation. Not one painting from the Hudson River school. Not a single goddamn pre-Columbian pot. Nothing. Whoever cleaned the museum out, did it with true professional style. Some soldiers stayed behind to occupy the facility. The helicopters came back for our teams, but in my opinion we had to claim a loss. We had taken back the facility, but all the art was gone. The Americans have been recovering these objects for the last few years, but there are many more out there, still undiscovered.

Chapter 12

RALLUJAH

European battalions had started out together from the north, traveling down I-95 from Delmarva, through Washington D.C., and finally down toward the Richmond Beltway. Those of us stationed in Norfolk travelled west along the I-64. Drone strikes continued to break up remaining checkpoints the Patriots had set up along the major roads. The small town of Ashland, just north of Richmond, put up only light resistance. The Americans dealt with it, and I didn't hear any shooting on most of our route along the I-64. Once we came within a few miles of the beltway though, snipers started to harass our convoy. Drones were deployed to make their situation untenable. There were no casualties at first, but these attacks became more frequent as we closed in. The tree line was so dense at the edge of the road that we didn't see the ambush waiting for us. Suddenly, from our right, bullets started raining down on the vehicles. Our gunners responded but, despite that, the enemy continued moving along the tree line, firing and moving. First one anti-tank round shot out, then another, leaving smoke trails behind them and large explosions from vehicles in the lead. At several points in our convoy, airburst grenades were fired into the trees, no doubt sending bark and shrapnel into the enemy line. As we used suppressing fire, the wounded and deceased were taken from the vehicles that had been hit. The majority of the convoy kept moving, which is almost always the best response to an ambush. A drone strike had been called for as soon as we encountered the enemy, but it wasn't until we had passed the worst point that I heard the sound of bombs and saw dark smoke clouds rising behind us. Those vehicles behind us continued firing grenades into the trees until ordered to stop. This process seemed to be repeated at every intersection and exit ramp from that point on.

Air support was invaluable in clearing most of the heavy equipment that could have presented the worst kinds of threat to us. The Americans still held the air, and the Patriots knew it. They would stay and engage us as long as they knew the skies were clear, but when they heard aircraft overhead (knowing what few they had were already downed) they often fled. The enemy that remained, we had to fight. At one point we braked. An Abrams tank and some infantry, which must have escaped the American sorties, got destroyed by some of the lead segments of our convoy. It had managed to surprise and destroy one Vamtac and damage another, but anti-tank rounds, along with 30mm and 40mm guns, turned it into a flaming wreck. The Patriots in Richmond seemed to favor close quarter ambushes, which could end up badly for either side. I'm not sure why they chose to go "toe-to-toe", as they say. There were fewer of them than there were of us, so a war of attrition didn't suit them. I can only guess that they assumed any citizens who roughly agreed with their generally Christian, right-wing, authoritarian bent would join them. People are not always as certain as they present themselves though, and it's a lot to assume that someone will leave their children to fight their own country for a dubious cause with faint odds of success. Anyone who shows up to that kind of fight is either a true believer, a mercenary, or a fool.

As soon as we took the exit for downtown, we took fire from a multistory open-air garage. The enemy opened up on us from several levels, and we did our best to suppress them. Since our path would only get harder the closer we got to the city center, several teams were ordered to take the garage. Hugo made the call, and we jumped out of our vehicle. The enemy started to shift fire toward anyone on foot, so we ducked and ran across the freeway and toward cover. There were several squads moving toward the garage under heavy fire. While some soldiers dropped into the median, which was recessed, those of us assaulting the garage looked for our opening. We were told to wait until a couple of our tanks could fire on the building. Several tank rounds struck the building near the top, rocking the ground - one, two, three, four, five. Airburst grenades, fired by other teams, were targeted to cover the roof. Hugo had ordered Sebastián and Miguel to fire anti-tank rounds into the top two levels of the garage, which were all good hits.

Smoke and dust drifted from the upper floors. Fire from the enemy grew more sporadic, and all of us began to move in, slowly, carefully. We were prone on the shoulder of the road, peeking out beneath the guard rail. Spread out as we were, our marksmanship really showed as we took aim and shot as many as we could. Several rifle teams were firing into the second and third floors, suppressing anyone who tried to fire at us. We managed to kill a number of them in this way, but the garage was segmented into three areas, so the walls protected some of them as they retreated. The first floor was intersected by the entry ramp, so we couldn't even see the other side.

The order had come down to clear the entire area, so we steeled ourselves for a long fight. Hugo rallied us, and we stormed down the embankment and ran for cover against the low concrete wall of the first floor. Two men kept firing, attempting to keep us pinned down. One was already injured and they had nowhere to go. Neva shot the uninjured man, dropping him quick. The sound was deafening, echoing off the concrete. Several of us put rounds into both men as we moved past. We could hear the sounds of the enemy footsteps reverberating down from the upper floors. As our teams flowed around a corner, a woman with red hair was trying to clear her rifle. She looked up at me, still ready to fight but caught with a jammed gun. Instead of pulling the trigger, I kicked her over like in that movie. Her head hit the concrete floor and she started convulsing. We zip-tied the woman and Neva stayed with her.

We cleared the next floor up, which was empty, and the next. Once we reached the second to last floor, the enemy threw two grenades at us. We backed off and took cover. Every time we thought they were done, more grenades came down the ramp, as if they had a never ending supply. Hugo got our attention to tell a story he had heard. He whispered it to us, "There was an airplane hijacking decades ago. A German response team entered the plane, but a terrorist tossed a grenade at them from the cockpit. When it exploded, the German screamed and screamed. The terrorist opened the door and poked his head out. The German put the pistol to the man's temple and pulled the trigger. What I'm saying is, I'm about to take some pretend shrapnel, everybody understand?" We all understood the play and nodded.

When the next grenade came down, Hugo started to scream like he'd just lost a foot. We all had our rifles trained on the concrete wall above, just waiting for anyone to poke their head up. All of a sudden, three Patriots leaned over the wall to look for their victim. We opened up on them, hitting a man and a woman in the head. The third, an older man, ducked away. There was no where to run, so we tossed some grenades of our own. I half expected they would try our own trick against us, but all we heard was silence.

The teams advanced in unison to clear both sides. There had actually been not three, but four Patriots left, and the grenades must have finished the other two off. The elderly man lay bleeding out. His chest rose and fell, faintly, but his eyes were closed. The girl looked to be less than 18 years old, stretched out behind some boxes, her shirt shredded and bloody. She could barely speak but she lifted her hands and looked at me plaintively. I leaned down to hear her whisper, "I'm already dead. I'm already dead." She seemed to be asking me not to harm her any further. I nodded and pulled out my IFAK to start treating her, but she died right there on the floor. From the level below I could hear the red-haired woman screaming, sobbing. I yelled down, "La Pelirroja? Neva, what's going on?" I couldn't understand what the woman was saying through her meltdown even after I made my way back, and it was useless asking. They were probably family; she must have felt when the girl died. Neva handed her off to others for questioning.

Several teams stormed another nearby garage and began to retake some office buildings which were only lightly defended. These we used together as a temporary combat outpost to begin retaking that section of the city. Dozens of soldiers ventured out on reconnaissance. The intelligence they gained would feed into our combat cloud, helping us locate enemy positions and fortifications. My team remained in the garage and spent our first night in Richmond on chilly concrete. The occasional crack of gunfire could be heard all around the city, but no one tested us. At least I had a good view of the stars. With others taking watch, I slept soundly through part of the night at least.

The next days ran one into another, with little sleep for two weeks. Most of our waking hours were consumed with clearing buildings and endless firefights. After good progress had already been made in the area, I remember my team running across a group of US Marines not far from the river. They were sheltering from the hot sun behind a building, some kneeling down, some hydrating. Hugo greeted them and asked how things were going. They said they were tasked with clearing defenses around the bridges over the James River. When we heard from one of the marines that his company had just finished capturing the American Civil War Museum from the Patriots, the irony was too rich to pass up. I quipped, "2-0, Civil War champions!"

He shot back, "Yeah, well they say that's the worst score in any sport. No time to get complacent, right?"

"I don't follow sport-ball, but it makes sense to me. Well done marines. See you back out there."

"Rah."

Chapter 13

REFORM

Once the guerrilla warfare had settled down, we moved into a brick building outside the city. One day, with nothing to do, I was talking to Hugo and Miguel on the patio when I brought up the idea of finding a leader for Richmond. Half joking, I suggested someone who would be strong enough to hold everything together, like a warlord. Hugo said a person like that would just use excessive force, which wouldn't help. The system needed legitimate authority, and reform, to come from the people. It is possible to change the mind of a person who holds radical ideas, but it's not enough. Only when the people agree to work through government will things get better. Of course I don't disagree with that but, to illustrate his point, Hugo told me a meandering story of his time in Africa. He said Miguel was there with him, during an operation in Mali.

"I was stationed in the Sahel. It was an all expense paid trip back to beautiful Mali, where sporadic struggle trees populate the landscape - all flat, dusty, red and yellow. I do appreciate the occasional rock formations though. This time around they wanted to send me in the rainy season, so that was interesting. It was scorching hot and despite the drought, sudden rains would come and

111

whip the trees while flooding everything. Perfect days for an al fresco lunch, am I right? Fucking August. Anyway, I got to practice my French, so that's something. Since we seemed to be everywhere in Africa even back then, I reminded myself that if I didn't like the weather I could wait awhile. There's always the next country.

"That was long after the Russians pulled out. The French went back in, and us with them. The Russians went too far in Africa anyway, and after forming a new government, they were smart to go home. Our mission in Mali was aligned with the French forces who were trying to prevent jihadist radicalization and respond to kidnappings and other unfortunate events. That and protect our commercial interests, like renewable energy projects. We wanted to create an environment to reduce recruitment and give the people a chance. Spain took a legalistic approach, so I worked with both our police and the local forces. Sometimes I worked with the help of the local citizens too. My role was to be a facilitator, a friendly ear, and the tip of the spear. At least I didn't have to train people on clearing landmines again. I had flexibility in that particular op so I really couldn't complain. We even got to dress down when we were trying to keep things quiet. I only had a handful of operators to back me up, which was plenty.

"So, I tracked a Mr. Ibrahim Kone, a.k.a. Ibn Omar, all through Bamako for weeks. At least Bamako is green; I miss trees when they're not around. I took a very nonchalant approach to my work back then; even I'll admit it. The thing is to know when you can. I would listen to music via a little ear bud hidden by a blue Tuareg tagelmust. No problem, since I usually had my comm in the other ear. Not the best disguise, but seeing as I have enough sangfroid for several men, this was the perfect time to listen to music. You know I love all kinds, so when I got back to Mali, I went down a rabbit hole of African music - psychedelic and high-life mostly, Orchestra Baobab especially.

Anyway, I guess I just try to view things as they really are. You start following a terrorist down some dusty side streets and graffiti covered mud-brick alleys, most operators are going to be tense and on high alert. Don't get me wrong, I have great situational awareness, but I don't blow things out of proportion. I mean, if this guy had tried to suddenly turn and shoot me, I figured I could pull the Mozambique drill on him before he finished turning around. Not to mention I knew he was unarmed, and alone. And my French is pretty damn good. Also, at the end of the day he's a smaller guy, probably a shitty fighter, out of shape, and a lot older than me. Los Viejos, am I right? I could have literally just grabbed him and beat the shit out of him in some back alley. But if you really want intelligence, you don't use harsh interrogation. Amateurs do that. I always find that if you ask a true believer he'll tell you. Oh, he'll tell you at length! And if he believes in something unprovable, the thing he fears most is not a gun, but his faith being shaken, finding out he's on the wrong side, having wasted his efforts, even his life, on the wrong ideals. So you just try to understand, listen, and be genuine. The reason most people don't succeed in interviews is they don't listen. That and they don't know fuck-all about anything *but* their job. A well rounded person can think for themselves and have a real dialogue.

"So back to Mr. Kone. I was following him on foot for quite a while. So even though I was hanging back, he really was pretty oblivious and overconfident for someone who proclaimed to lead a new band of Islamist terrorists. His security people obviously failed to make an impression on him, but I guess he figured varying his path wherever he went would be enough. I almost felt bad as I watched him look around every time he had to make a turn, as if he barely knew where he was anymore. Did I mention we kept eyes on him with tiny drones at all times? Each one only lasted a half hour but they were small and cheap enough to keep at least one up constantly. Like I said, when you stop to think about it, a power imbalance should give you pause, allow you to stay calm, rather than devolve into sloppy and violent reactionary behavior. We can all shit on everything that moves if we have to, right? As I followed him up another alley, a beautiful white barb horse tied to a wall distracted me. In the light though, he almost looked golden. It makes sense looking back on it because we were not far from the Hippodrome. This song Guajira Van was playing through my earbud, and I remember thinking – if this goes terribly, terribly wrong, I'm riding off on that fucking horse to this song. Ah, the things that amuse me. Mr. Kone was nearly about to make another fucking bumble-turn when I decide to make my move.

"He might have heard me walking just a little faster than everyone else, but he didn't. I let Miguel know to fall back because I wanted to talk to our friend over dinner. I heard him sigh and he says 'see you back at the chalet'. So I closed in on our Mr. Kone and gently touched his elbow. Pulling my veil down I said: "We need to talk". He opened his mouth but didn't know what to say, so I immediately went on. "I'm one of the foreign soldiers here to track down terrorists, but you look like you could use dinner rather than a game of tag with us. Let's sit down and get some dinner, my treat. Then we can talk." He looked extremely worried but at least agreed to go with me. I suggested a great nearby restaurant that I knew which served halal food, plus we could eat outside. He said he had eaten there before and seemed to relax just a little. I asked him what he ordered before and if he liked it. He said it had been a very long time and he didn't remember. We made small talk as we walked. I noticed he was fidgeting a little and I wanted him to relax, so I told him we were going to order whatever we want because someone else was paying it for tonight. This made him smile a little. So I said, 'Please forgive my disguise, maybe I could have put in more effort'. He relaxed when we approached the restaurant. The waiter came and we agreed to sit outside. It was actually shaping up to be a nice afternoon as far as weather goes, not too hot. We had an umbrella over our table and a large shade tree over that. I think we ordered everything on the menu.

Hugo went on. "As we ate we talked about where we grew up, our religious upbringing, our parents, and so on. I raised the issue of my being an atheist which seemed to horrify him a bit, but I explained that it's not like you choose - it's more like you can no longer believe in something once you understand it's not real. His wrinkled his nose at me, which pushed his wire-framed glasses up a little. He raised the prospect of me going to hell, but I told him that at the end of the day, no one knows, and it's all our opinion, superstition, and guesswork. All signs point to death being the end, so it really matters what we do with our life. He seemed rigidly opposed to this idea but suggested if that were true, nothing would matter. I retorted, "That's not true, because it matters to *us* ". Sure the universe doesn't care, but it's only sad when we don't care about each other as we should". Then I asked him what the transformative moment was for his journey in Islam. He didn't hesitate. He described being a young man and going off to wage jihad against "America" and "The West" because they were in the Muslim world. But I asked him why - was he always interested in politics, and what got him to pay attention. He described hearing about innocent lives lost, shops and towns destroyed, the violent tug of war between various factions and foreign armies, and the endless hopelessness that all this chaos caused. So I suggested, "You're saying that the Americans and Western Countries, as well as the warlords and factions, they fought but did not stop to try to understand each other? That before understanding, they fought? And those innocent people caught in the middle, they just wanted to live their lives. No wonder everything falls apart without understanding. Misunderstandings can lead to conflict. If only they had been patient and talked to each other, as we are. As they say, first, do no harm.

I asked, "But what did you say to get him to reconsider?

Hugo thought a moment. "I talked about his people. I said, 'It's not too late for you Ibrahim. And it wasn't too late for Mohamed either. He's only 16. I talked him out of it. I've been talking to him for a little while now. And Issa's out too.' I started to see defeat creep up on his face. He asked me if I was going to kill him. I told him 'No, but you've walked into a spotlight that I don't know if you can ever step out of again. I know you've been to prison before, and I'm sure you'd rather not go back. To be honest, we really want your competitors. The way I see it, if you were to simply tell your people you're stepping down and they should too…I think that would help. We could work together. This thing hasn't gone too far, yet. Are you strong enough to get them to do that? There are many ways to resolve conflicts and protect people that don't involve killing. The problems you see are not about religion, and neither are the solutions. These are legal and political issues, and maybe we can help. People need food, water, peace, justice, and freedom from corruption. As a citizen, let's refocus your energy on the public good. Leave fighting to the armies, and keep your eye on the government who's supposed to be watching out for the people. Raise your voices, not your guns. Religion is not the reason you deserve a just world, *that you're alive is*. In this, we can help you – let your people know. Let us help, and you can help us to unravel the plans of those who really have gone too far. You only have this one life on earth, and if you want to truly help people, then you'll do it the right way…the right way, Ibrahim.' That's what I told him.

"He stared down at his plate and even seemed to be tearing up a little. Just when he looked back up, he nodded and was going to say something, but the waiter came to ask if we were finished, interrupting us, just lingering awkwardly. It did lighten the mood a bit and Mr. Kone laughed at the waiter, nervously. I paid the waiter well more than the bill, in part just to make his nosy ass go away. Once he left, I let Mr. Kone know that since we could easily monitor him, I'd just choose to trust him for now and we could stay in touch. I wished him the best and was about to shake his hand when

118

two shots rang out from behind the fence, and I immediately whipped around to return fire (since I still had my sidearm). I only heard someone running away, and then yelling from beyond the fence, probably from the restaurant staff. I turned back to see Mr. Kone slumping, one shot to his side, not fatal. He said he knew he was going to die. I smiled, put my hand on his shoulder, and told him, 'Nonsense, no one gets off that easy in life'. He groaned but smiled a little, and I put pressure on the wound until one of the wait staff took over. I yelled to get an ambulance. I noticed our waiter was nowhere to be seen, probably tipped someone off. There was nothing else I could do in the restaurant, so I ran out of the seating area and jumped the fence. People who were standing around outside pointed me in the direction the shooter had gone. I ran up the narrow street they pointed to and, after a good distance, realized I was right back near the area where I had first found Mr. Kone. I didn't see anyone at all, so I tried to listen for footsteps. Hearing nothing, I called in to Miguel to let him know what happened and that I'd be back soon, depending on if I could locate the shooter. It wasn't long before I could hear a small mob coming down from the side street, shouting "Allahu Akbar!" I peeked around the corner and saw a bunch of the future former Ibn Omar crew closing in fast. Given that one of them might have had a gun, I decided to get out of there. Better to see if the group could be unraveled peacefully. That's when I remembered the

119

horse. I ran like a track star to find the area where he was tied up. After searching a couple of alleys I actually found the right one. There he was, the white barb horse, just looking at me. Of course, I'm normally no horse thief but I commandeered it, only temporarily, and only out of necessity! I untied him, jumped up, and this horse was fucking surprised, but when I say he was fast, ¡Maldita sea! It put a big smile on my face to ride so fast, and I called Miguel to tell him where to pick me up. I may or may not have listened to Guajira Van as I rode! I raced that horse for maybe three kilometers before letting him rest. I took it a bit slower the rest of the way, until I reached the meeting place. Miguel was there with a Vamtac and a couple of soldiers to pick me up."

Miguel jumped in at this point in the story, "Hey dude, were you *trying* to get us killed that night? This motherfucker", Miguel said, nodding at Hugo. "We laughed when he showed up on a horse. He just dismounted, then pulled a serious face at the horse, pointed back at the town, all stern and shit, and yelled, 'Return to base!' That horse took off *like lightning*. We fucking lost it. On the way back he told us the whole story. We were shaking our heads. Man, you must be the luckiest guy I've ever met."

Hugo went on, shrugging it off with a smile, "Hey, if I don't keep you on your toes, who will? Anyway, we got a couple of CNP and local guys to guard Mr. Kone at the hospital. He lived. We hid his associates in the safe house. Mission accomplished."

I thought a moment and shot back, "Wait, what was the point of that long ass story?"

Looking back to me more seriously, he added, "I felt like maybe I did some real *good* on that trip. But then the government gradually improved, the economy got better, and a lot of the issues just…went away. That's the real moral of the story. We were just barely maintaining the status quo. I started to see how all of this fighting is not what makes things better, not really. It just cleans up the messes. That's necessary, and without it the world does sort of fall apart, but it's not enough. Individuals can't fix everything by themselves; it has to be the people, together. It has to be the whole system. That's why this time around, America, these government reforms, *have to work*. We need to buy the Americans enough time so the new system can take hold. If they double down on democracy, and put one foot in front of the other, it will."

Chapter 14

CAPTIVES

Once the Patriots had been cleared out of Richmond, along with the local militias, we started to hear of local gangs trying to fill the vacuum. This was especially true south of the James River, in Jackson Ward. We received intelligence gathered from contacts in every region we travelled through, usually during routine interviews. At this time, however, we had several people ask to speak to NATO forces stationed in and around Richmond, asking for help. This had always happened, but there were so many small operations they seemed never-ending. One morning we were told of a man who had talked to Spanish soldiers at a checkpoint. Something about a gang. I felt ill at that time and although I protested, Hugo ordered me to see the medic. Not that I have anything against Martín, but I was not worried and didn't want to be away. Just as I thought, he said it was likely something I ate. Martín gave me some antacids and sent me on my way. Hugo had taken a team and picked up this local man so we could interview him further. I came back just as they were bringing him in, and I was glad I didn't miss much.

Volunteering myself to help with the interview, I listened while Ben asked the questions. Hugo sat back and listened too, since Ben had a very nonthreatening demeanor during interviews. People opened up to him, in a different way than they did with me. Americans seemed to view me as challenging, someone to guard themselves against. I probably held eye contact too long, they find that unnerving. The informant told Ben to call him "Chalky". He was a man in his 20s, with long hair and an unkempt hippie vibe. He smelt of patchouli, and in my mind I kept waiting for him to end a sentence with "myaaan". An admission of drug use made us wary, but he seemed clear at the time, and his story was believable. He told us that he lived in a duplex, but the landlord had moved out at the beginning of the troubles in Richmond and hadn't been back, or even contacted him for rent, so he had both apartments to himself. He let acquaintances stay with him sometimes too, and it turns out one of them had gang affiliations. Recently, the man he was allowing to live next door brought several friends to stay. They were all members of a gang called The 13s. This had made Chalky nervous, because they were armed and loud. The day before, he heard the voices of young girls, followed by crying. It got so bad that he knocked on the door. One of the men threatened him with a weapon, so he went back to his apartment. He said he lay awake all night, terrified, listening to the women being yelled at and brutalized. He tried to report the issue to local police but they never responded. Any local police remaining were likely running protection rackets or busy saving their own lives by staying out of trouble. That is what led him to seek us out: desperation.

We first tried to reach out to local police, since we'd eventually need to work with them anyway. We had hoped to build local capabilities through training, and even seek assistance while making arrests of higher value targets. There was no local response to our calls. As Ben interviewed Chalky, Hugo decided to check on the state of the local police. He sent Sebastián to the precinct to see if he could talk to anyone and then radio us, but he discovered only one lone cop hiding there, vest on and uniform off. There were bullet holes throughout each room, and many doors were still smashed in. This cop was no help, and was merely using the precinct as a shelter and stockpile for the duration of this minor apocalypse. There was no authority there. This put the gang problem back in our laps.

We made a few phone calls to notify the authorities so they could re-allocate cops. Then we talked to the US Army and our commanders – under martial law, they assured us we could proceed with a small operation to capture or kill the gang once we had established that violent felonies were being committed. Sex trafficking and rape are, of course, felonies. Uncle Sam asked us to proceed. We just needed to surveil the house, and Chalky could help us with that. We asked him to sit tight and keep talking to Ben while we went into another room to discuss.

As we discussed the situation, a plan emerged. We'd use two teams, an alpha and beta, along with a k-9 handler and a sniper outside. Once we had a look inside the house with thermal imaging and handheld radar, we'd attempt a peaceful check to defuse any illegal activity and make arrests if necessary. If the gang fired on us, or had hostages, we were free to respond with all necessary force. The main goal, however, was to verify that women were being held against their will, and if so, to get them out. A cheap burner phone was set up for this purpose and logged.

Re-entering the interview room, we asked Chalky if he was still willing to help us, even if it meant going back into his apartment. He said, "Yeah, but like, what if they ask where I went?"

Ben told him, "Chalky, they have no reason to suspect you. Other than sticking a gun in your face, it could be more suspicious if you *didn't* return. Don't you think?"

"Yeah, I guess."

"Ok" Ben said, "then do you think you can ask to speak to your acquaintance? If you can peek in the room when he opens the door, let us know what you see. Ask about the girls, as if you're interested. Text the details to us on this phone", Ben said, sliding the burner across the table. Chalky agreed, but I could see he was nervous.

As we gathered the team, we fed Chalky and did our best to reassure him. Rafael, who was an excellent soldier from one of our other teams, joined us for this op. Once everything was ready and we had designated a highly recommended canine handler (whose name was José), one of our snipers, Pablo, and his spotter Simón, we loaded up and set out. It did not escape me that the dog walking slowly past me toward the APC was a Spanish mastiff. It had a variegated grey coat and thick muscles; a drooling monster with a thick leather collar and an unnerving stare. His light brown eyes coldly locked onto us as he hopped up into the vehicle. José kept him close, for which I was very thankful. He even handed Chalky a treat to give to the dog. That seemed to soften the big dog's mood a bit. Luckily for the gang members, the dog was only there to catch anyone fleeing on foot. I don't want to see what he could have done to a human being.

Chalky told us where it was safe to let him out. We pulled behind a pair of burnt out houses. One of them was painted robin's egg blue with a gaping hole into the kitchen. Chalky hopped out alone, walking into the murky shell that used to be someone's home. There was still a little fake plant on the kitchen windowsill, untouched somehow. This location was a distance from Chalky's house, but he had given us the layout of the neighborhood along with the locations of any other houses that might tip off the 13s gang. It was better that he not be seen with us.

We waited for a long time, but that's most of a soldier's job. Eventually Chalky texted us, Miguel

126

read it aloud, and texted back our consensus. It was a good thing that we did not have anyone in view, because the 13s had pulled a gun on Chalky again and backed him right off the porch. They told him he needed to leave his apartment before they shot him right there. I think he said their exact words were, "Pack your shit and get the fuck out". He said he would grab a few things and never come back. His so-called acquaintance wouldn't see him or even intervene. Chalky did see into the living room, and there were more women than before, a couple with black eyes and bruises. He said he counted four or five armed men in view, talking with each other. He guessed all of them were at least armed with pistols, and two definitely had AR-15s.

After talking it through, we decided to send a micro-drone to look in the windows and verify who and what was inside. Miguel had the control tablet and described what he saw. Most of the windows had been covered up and some reinforced. From what he could see, Chalky's observations checked out. Several gunmen were guarding an unknown number of women, who were being held in small groups throughout the house. From one of Chalky's windows, Miguel described a large mouse hole in the wall. Apparently, on the second floor, the 13s had recently kicked a rough entrance between the two apartments. Normally, we would enter from the roof or an upper floor, but since the hole appeared fresh and no one was occupying Chalky's side yet, we decided to take advantage of having an empty staging point next door with near-silent access. Plus, they did just tell him to "pack his shit", so if they heard anything they'd probably hesitate a bit. We got the key from Chalky and prepared for entry by his back door.

We formed an A team and a B team, with a sniper team on overwatch. I was on A-team, which Hugo led. Hugo and Rafael both had shotguns, while Neva and I still had our HKs. B-team, under Miguel, was set up the same. I took point for A-team. After twilight, we walked in single file, moving through abandoned buildings to mask our movement. Using the thermal setting on our night vision, we moved slowly and quietly to make sure we were not seen. Slow is smooth, smooth is fast. Approaching the yellow duplex, we went to the right until we came to a small, paved back yard. Rafael quietly unlocked Chalky's back door. I held the door open as everyone made their way in. In the dark, we silently went from the living room, past the kitchen, to the stairs. We moved very slowly up the wooden stairs, walking nearer to the wall to prevent squeaking. Near the top of the stairs I marked the hallway and three bedrooms. We could hear the neighbors, and the second floor had some light entering from the hole in the wall. Using two man teams, we cleared the rooms in no time. I kept my eye on the last bedroom. In the last bedroom on the right, the master, was the mouse hole, an oval about five feet high on our left upon entering the room. A light was on in the other apartment, and we could hear crosstalk; a number of raised voices amid an argument.

Using our goggles, we could see that there were 8 women and five gunmen, all downstairs. The second floor had no thermal signatures. We decided to quietly enter through the hole, and then flood down into the first floor of the other apartment to catch the 13s while they were arguing. We readied flash-bangs and crept through the mouse hole. As we were coming down the stairs, I saw four of the women, girls really, sitting on a couch. One of the girls looked up to see me, and although masked, I put my finger over my lips. She looked scared, but put her finger over her own lips to quiet the other girls, shifting her eyes toward us as we descended. Their silence was tense. Moving toward the kitchen, we knew the 13s were focused on their argument. The four other girls were eating at a kitchen table behind the 13s. They were cornered. Hugo pointed to Rafael and himself, and they moved closer to the kitchen entry. He pointed to Neva and I to come in after. Rafael grabbed a flash-bang from Hugo's pack. Hugo nodded, and Rafael threw it in. Immediately following the boom, Hugo slid along the kitchen wall so we were at a 90-degree angle from the girls, and Rafael followed like they were glued together. They fired their shotguns into the gang before they could even react, and Neva and I moved in to fire into the downed bodies of the 13s. The girls were screaming over the gunfire, until Hugo held up his hand to cease-fire. In just a couple of seconds, it was all over. We made sure to ask the girls if there was anyone else, but it was clear.

Neva doubled back to help the B-team with the girls in the living room, and I brought out the four girls from the kitchen. There was also a C and D team outside providing security. We questioned the girls briefly and found out that there were multiple houses. I remember one of the girls had a round face with one eye swollen shut, a caramel complexion and curly, dark hair. She said her name was Olivia, and she asked me about her sister who had been taken to another house. She was crying, and kept repeating "…my sister…". I made a promise to her that we would get every girl out, including her sister. We walked the girls out the front door and into the APCs. Chalky went back to his apartment to gather his things, but I believe he went north soon after. Once we got back to base, the girls were fed, allowed to clean up, and given fresh clothes. We turned the operation over to the Army's MOE (Mando de Operaciones Especiales), since they would be able to take the entire gang out. And that they did. MOE essentially decimated the 13s gang in Richmond, with dozens killed or arrested. The last thing every member of that gang probably heard was a breaching charge. Each house occupied by the 13s was raided, and weapons, drugs, and a number of other girls were found, including Olivia's older sister Ava. Promises kept.

Chapter 15

CLOSE

Now, Olivia's sister Ava had a friend who had been trafficked at the same house in Hillside Court. Her name was Charlotte. I went and met all of these girls when they were brought back to base. We let them choose new clothes that had been donated from other parts of the country, and I remember one she picked out - a colorful floral sundress. Charlotte had blond hair and was fairly tall at 5'10". In fact, she told me her brother, who was a couple of years older and several inches taller, had played high school basketball. Her brother, Mike, was the only one left at home because their father, a guardsmen, had been killed by the Patriots. We had someone pick Mike up and bring him in, given the unusual circumstances. Charlotte was understandably furious about what had happened to her and talked about revenge in excruciating detail. But when she was calmed, she had lambent eyes and I saw that she could have done many things in life; they all could have. I tried my best to befriend these kids, and let them talk about whatever they wanted. I just wanted to be there to listen. They stayed with us for a period of time, and while MOE was clearing all of the houses, their numbers grew. Although we had vouchsafed their freedom, a plot to avenge themselves formed.

One day Charlotte pulled me aside and whispered, "We're going to Petersburg – me, my brother, and Ava. We're going to kill the man who killed my father. He's one of the leaders of the Patriots. They served together a long time ago, and he shot my dad because they had all these arguments. I know it had to be him, or his fucking guys."

"Charlotte, join the military when you're old enough, but please don't do anything now."

"My mind's made up", she said.

"Please tell me what you know. Maybe we can find this person."

"His name is Doug Hahn. I told you, he's high up, like a general."

I asked her, "What sort of man is he?"

Charlotte replied, "He's a jizz-head".

"A what?"

"Like, an asshole. He thinks he's right all the time, even when he's not. He's mean, he has a temper, and he acts like a fucking cult member, just like a lot of these Patriot guys. They are so sure they're right. They don't care who they have to fuck over, as long as they get their way. I mean, just look around. And…he killed my dad." Charlotte glared at me.

I said nothing. There was nothing I could share, so I told her we'd look into it. It seemed to me that she left it in our hands because she gave a slight nod and walked away. However, after a week or so, the three of them disappeared. We had no way to track them down, and they were free to go, but I feared the worst. I asked around about them. Apparently, the general had her father killed around Thanksgiving the year before. Her father and General Hahn had indeed served together in the military, just as she said. They had even grown up together as friends. Speaking to a number of civilians, and putting together information gathered by all of us who were looking for Hahn, we knew that there were several places they might show up. We knew that it would all depend on the general sticking his head up though.

The Patriots converged on several spots in Petersburg, but one in particular caught our attention. Fleeing south from Richmond on the I-95, a portion of the enemy gathered in force at a defunct mall. The Patriots still held Petersburg but they were looking to defend it. It would only make sense that the general might want to personally direct the defenses before leaving. Enemy forces shelled Richmond, which was already in terrible shape, destroying some of the remaining buildings. Between houses burnt to the ground, office buildings with every window blown out, and concrete mottled with every shade of black and grey, it is no wonder the city had earned the moniker Rallujah. Petersburg was a smaller city of three and sometimes four story brick buildings, and not very dense. Still, there would have been plenty of places to snipe at our soldiers. At that time, NATO forces had air superiority, especially through drones, and used that fact to good effect by bombing every enemy vehicle they could spot, including many near the mall. I was not involved with the general siege of Petersburg, but when we started getting intel that Hahn was in fact at the mall, we devised a plan to take several helicopters and capture him.

Before we could act, at around nine in the morning, we got a report of a massive explosion at a mall. We set out in the early afternoon by helicopter. The thinking was, we had not caused the blast, perhaps it was an accident involving an ammo dump, or even terrorism, but the confusion might provide good cover. On approach we saw an ominous black cloud rising from the mall. Due to the ongoing fire, we roped in near the edge of a parking lot. Bits of debris were scattered everywhere. There was no resistance at all. The side of the mall had completely collapsed in one whole section. This is where the fire was concentrated. Smoke was driven into our faces by slow eddies of wind. Crumpled cars, Humvees, and other military vehicles sat smoldering, their paint destroyed by the heat.

Off to the right of the destruction, a small pile of bodies had been stacked next to the wall. Judging by the smell, some were starting to be consumed by fire and we could hear it crackle mockingly. I had no plan to linger, but something caught my eye. The corpses were civilians, young men and women. The bare feet of a young girl protruded from the pile, the edge of her colorful dress morbidly curling upward by a spreading flame. As I approached, I remembered the floral pattern. It was the same dress we had given Charlotte when we first brought her back to base. I rolled one of the young men off to expose her, wincing as I did. Although she had been shot in the face it was Charlotte, her hair soaked in blood. I looked to Neva, and she helped me smother the flames and lay the bodies out. Aside from Charlotte, Ava and Mike were there, along with a couple of other young men. They had all been shot. We cleared the area, then radioed in for the army to take control of the entire shopping district and collect the bodies of the kids. If Hahn had been there he might have been killed by the blast, but then who had killed the teens, and what had they done? I wished we had found them before, but I know they would not have listened to our counsel.

Once we returned to base, I contacted Olivia. She cried a little, but not as much as I expected. Olivia went on to explain the whole plan, and said that she hoped the General was finally dead. The plan had been to use a truck bomb to make sure. Once they heard gossip that Hahn was at the mall, they made an agreement. Charlotte would have driven the truck with Ava in the passenger seat, both dressing provocatively. They would charm their way past any guards, and try to park it pointed toward the target for maximum damage. Mike and his friends were hidden in the back, in large boxes. It was supposed to look like it was full of medicine, alcohol, and food in case anyone checked. They could jump out and assault any guards or other opposition before getting away and detonating the bomb. Charlotte was supposed to act dumb, and ask for Hahn by name at the checkpoint, saying some local "friends" sent her to welcome the general. The Patriots would no doubt have checked the contents of the truck, but would have seen it as supplies. None of the teen's bodies were badly burned, so they must have avoided the explosion. The two girls would have been told to exit the vehicle, of course. A driver might have taken the truck into the mall parking lot to unload. The rest could only be pieced together. Since the boys were not burned but the truck destroyed, they obviously made it out. In fact, the truck exploded in a massive fireball, as we all heard, sending clouds of dust and debris in every direction. I imagine the kids tried to put up resistance but stood no chance against so many men.

In Petersburg, the Patriots put up fierce opposition but were defeated over the course of several days with lots of air support. The marines cleared houses and the army held ground. We formed checkpoints and started to restore order. The enemy had seemed to melt back into the landscape, along with much of the remaining equipment we had failed to destroy. No doubt civilian sympathizers helped them. Local bases reported back that all was relatively quiet following

Petersburg. None of us trusted that to last. We put out feelers among the citizens for any information on General Hahn, but there were only rumors. Rumors were going around that he'd be back, that he was close, or that he was already dead, and none of it sat well with us. It was all so vague.

Once Petersburg had finally fallen silent for several days, I recall a moment of surreal calm. We were driving back from a quiet patrol and it was a beautiful day. The sun was shining and it was full summer. Hugo had his high life music playing as we listened in our own contented silences. One of the songs was Nri Sport Di Uso, and I was watching wild bamboo pass endlessly as we drove. Yes it's invasive, but I love it. The windows were rolled down a little and I took off my boonie hat to let my hair blow around. I felt relaxed and safe, like we were all young again, just hanging out. I felt like maybe we had seen the worst of it and allowed myself to pass into a trance-like joy. And the bamboo rolled by.

Chapter 16

SUMMER CAMP

NATO forces had taken and prepared an advance airfield a little west of Petersburg. This was established at Dinwiddie Airport. While Spanish Army engineers from the 11th were helping to rebuild in Richmond and Petersburg, they were also at work with sappers to expand the runway, add buildings and create more lots. American engineers arrived to assist and plan, which led to a greatly expanded site, suitable for military use. American soldiers continued to pour in, bolstering our numbers. It was no longer just a forward airfield, but not exactly a major air base either. The central location allowed us to start controlling the main roads in the area. The Americans on base now seemed sure Hahn had indeed escaped the blast at the mall, and would try to counterattack. We met several Army Rangers wandering around one day who told us about some intel suggesting Hahn was alive. Supposedly it was verified with multiple independent sources, so that was that. We all agreed we needed to keep up the hunt, or he'd slip away and regroup again.

During the afternoon of the next day, a couple of the Rangers we met the day before drove us around in a four door armored pickup truck. One of them, a likeable Staff Sergeant named Alan Rye, explained that he was raised in the area. The other soldier, a younger man named John Lin, said he had recently come in fresh from Washington State, this being his first deployment. He said he'd mostly been hanging around base and wanted to get outside the fence again. Clearly, he wanted to see some action. Lin shared how he had been on patrol just days earlier, when they found Rye alone, hungry and filthy. Apparently the other soldiers from Rye's patrol were MIA. Rye said he had gotten separated from his team during an ambush outside Petersburg and hid out for three days with very little to eat, afraid to move around. He and Lin had struck up a fast friendship and had mostly been wandering around on base, bored.

Finally, the day before, Lin said they were allowed to do recon West along the 460 but encountered no opposition. Since the road had seemed clear, Rye said he'd heard rumors about a small prison camp being set up in an abandoned set of buildings a bit further than they'd driven. He had been to a place like that a long time ago, a spot he and his friends would go to drink as teenagers. So Rye told Lin that's where Hahn might go. Lin cut in to agree with the idea - local rumors had it that Hahn may have retreated with a core group to hide out, but that he was staying relatively close after Petersburg fell. The bulk of the Patriot forces had likely melted into the population for now, but that could change. This would allow them to determine if a counter-attack was possible. Rumors also said that the Patriots had started gathering intelligence by interrogating military prisoners somewhere nearby, so to Rye the location made perfect sense.

Since we didn't want anything to leak, we let base know we'd be doing a short bit of recon for a possible enemy position. Rye seemed excited, and suggested we just do a little "sneak and peek", and that a main Ranger assault team could take care of the rest. Lin seemed a little unsure, but agreed it should be safe enough along the road to go at least a little farther than the day before. The drive took longer than Rye had described, but he insisted on pressing ahead until we passed the point he and Lin had reached. We started to question whether we should turn around, but he explained that he thought he knew the place – it was likely an old summer camp he went to as a child. Since he thought he knew the way to the camp he suggested we'd park off road, and then safely approach from the woods to get a good view of the camp. The idea was to travel relatively light and fast. Relying on his knowledge of the area, we agreed only to do a little light recon but avoid any possibility of contact. We didn't want to alert the Patriots, or any militia who might be on good terms with them.

Once we reached the place and pulled off the road, Rye said to Lin that they should go together and we could stay with the vehicle. They set off into the woods and we waited near the vehicle in a tiny clearing. After an hour or so, we heard the two rangers making their way back.

Lin said, "It's there, for sure. We didn't even get close but it actually seems to be a big complex with a lot of men. It was hard to see through the trees since we didn't want to get too close, but we could hear all the activity." Rye nervously said that based on what little they observed, he had radioed in to advise that a force of Rangers should assault the compound and to await instruction. He apologized and said they probably should have observed a bit more. We agreed that this was all a bit thin, since based on what little they had observed there was a danger of sending too small a team or not having the proper support. Hugo and I suggested doing a bit more recon, but with all four of us. We could split into two groups, and if it was safe, we might get a fuller idea of the layout, men, and equipment before it was too dark. Once we met back up and compared notes, then we could radio in more accurate positions, numbers, defenses, and so on. It might be better to strike later anyway, since the assault teams would all have night vision with access to CC.

Staff Sergeant Rye said he fully agreed with that plan so we moved out. We passed closer to the forest edge as it slowly sloped down from the oaks and pines. As we finally got close we could hear some commotion. The forest gently sloped back down toward what could faintly be seen past the trees - roads, vehicles and men. Rye radioed in the Ranger assault, saying it was a go. We heard him listen for a second then sign off. Of course we were completely taken aback, since we had not really observed much more than he and Lin had seen. He abruptly told us the main Ranger force was not too far behind us, and seeming to anticipate our concerns, suggested that we move up a little and do some better recon before the main force arrived. His plan was to then fall back and connect with the main assault team prior to any action being taken.

We reluctantly agreed only to do a little more observation before pulling back. Rye then immediately started off to the right, pointing over to the left where he said he and Lin had been earlier. Hugo and I crawled quietly down toward the compound, which had decent cover with all the shrubs and weeds at the forest edge. Using binoculars we had a good view through the foliage, even though some concrete abutments and walls obscured some of our view. What we observed past a perimeter road seemed to be a full military base. It was definitely *not* a summer camp. Convoys of military vehicles could be seen on the move. There was no question this was the place, and with all the activity and manpower we determined to immediately retreat back into the forest.

Suddenly four guards hidden nearby in camouflaged blind spots manage to shoot us both at point blank range, which was thankfully stopped by our body armor. They grabbed ahold of us, practically before we could hit the ground. Hugo, who also had a bullet graze his throat, pretended to be unconscious, and I wonder if the trickle of blood forming across his neck might be what saved us. Clouds had gathered as the evening came. Given how far we were from the floodlights, and how dark the sky was getting, this was enough. I'm sure it helped that I had hit my cheek on a rock and also had some blood trickling down.

As they picked me up and dragged me toward a low, white building, more men came up to grab us. I turned my head to see Hugo being dragged by the arms until they set him down for a better grip. The instant they set him down he leapt up and made quick work of the two men with his knife. More soldiers were running up toward us. No sooner had he cut the two men down, he grabbed his gun and disappeared back into the dark woods in the blink of an eye. I remember him glancing back at me just before blending into the dark, and I knew not to fear.

The soldier on my right arm, a thin blond man with a beard, yelled out, "Fuck! He ran into the woods!" I heard several men moving in the direction Hugo had gone, followed by several shots from AR-15s. After a pause, I heard shots from an HK. My two captors dragged me inside the white building and, slamming the door, pushed me down so hard onto a cheap metal chair that it shifted, loudly. The screech of the metal grating against the floor was deafening. The lighting was dim and fluorescent; the walls were painted in grubby white, like some cheap garage. The floor was simple un-swept concrete, with traces of large bloodstains everywhere, making it look like some ancient map of the known world. The two soldiers smirked and set my gun against the wall near them. They had pulled my pack off and started to root through it for valuables. I didn't react. Outside, I could hear men shouting.

An interrogator burst into the room almost immediately, walked right up to me, and slapped me hard across the face. He was a big, bearded man with a fat belly, loud, and very angry. There were a couple of other men who followed him in. I looked back at him with no expression, and he just glared back. Then he screamed at me "Who are you? What are you doing here bitch?" I just looked down and stayed quiet. He grabbed my hair and pulled me closer, "How many of you are there? Look at me, look me in the eye".

I spoke in a thick accent, slowly, quietly, and without making eye contact "We help to work with the water, sir".

"Bullshit!" he boomed, and threw my head back, making the chair click against the floor.

I calmly stated, "Sir, I am from Spain, and I am a water specialist". Glancing up at him I said, "I got lost and don't even want to be here". After that I just started fumbling my English and rambling. I even looked to the other two soldiers as though I was trying to convince all of them. The reality is I was trying to memorize everything about my environment and about them. The two men who had followed the interrogator in had mismatched gear and no true uniforms, which let me know that they were militia. The guards who had captured me, on the other hand, were Patriots. There was another man in regular army uniform who entered to observe, and was taking notes over his reading glasses from a chair in the back. I didn't dwell on it at the time, but the shoulder patch on his uniform was one I hadn't seen before – an arrowhead inscribed with with a capital "T".

It felt like a very long time to me, even though this was probably very short for an interrogation. As I was avoiding questions and dragging out every response my interrogator shot me an angry look and leaned in again to slap me. He opened his mouth, baring his teeth, and then his expression dropped. He jerked backwards, looking up and over my head, and his face suddenly exploded onto mine. Hugo had slipped up to the entrance, cracked the door, and shot the interrogator. He then shot the two soldiers standing over my backpack before they knew where the shots were coming from. I leapt toward the door while grabbing my weapon and ran outside to provide cover. Hugo stepped back outside and dropped in a flash-bang; he stepped back in and shot the two militiamen again. As he kept the weapon trained on the man in the back, who had half fallen out of his chair, I slipped back in and grabbed my pack.

Hugo looked at the man and demanded, "Where's Hahn?"

The guy just slowly looked to his right, toward the door, as a silent signal. He started to stammer something in awful Spanish with what sounded like a fake Mexican accent. I believe he was starting to ask us to wait, to let him go. Hugo immediately shot him twice in the chest and one in the head. "Time to go!" he said jauntily.

We raced out of there as quietly as we could. As we jumped the low concrete wall, we heard shouts and running. As we made our way deeper into the woods, I saw where Hugo had killed two additional men and dragged all four into the bushes, as one does. We pushed on, determined to escape.

"Did the Rangers make it?" I asked.

"Yes, they're just ahead – they pulled back" he whispered.

As we picked our way back through the small trees though, we dimly saw a lone figure in a clearing sprawled out on the ground. The left hand was covering the neck. Sadly, this dead figure was Lin, who we had just been with a short time before. His body would need to be recovered, so I fixed our location. It looked like he had been stabbed in the side of the neck, and blood was soaking the leaves below. Otherwise, the forest floor was barely disturbed and the attack seemed to have been from behind. His right hand was stretched up and out toward his left, as though reaching. Lin's face looked angry but defiant, as though he had still won. Following the angle of his arm, the leaves were barely disturbed, meaning the walker meant to leave no trace. Still, a few feet away we found sign that a single person had separated from the path the rangers had been traveling. It made sense. Rye was a traitor, and we had been set up and betrayed.

I said: "If Rye reaches Hahn's forces, he'll give away anything he can. He was on base for days. We have to find him now, or lose him."

His dry response was: "Seek and destroy".

Since this supposed Ranger was now moving fast in the dark he left a lot more sign, and we could hear him ahead of us. We chased Sergeant Rye through the gentle hills of those woods and managed to catch up as he was starting to near the Patriot lines again. Once we saw that he was only about 100 meters ahead of us we knew we had to strike. He was running downhill; sliding and stumbling in the leaves, ready to run up the next hill and across to where Patriots were likely standing guard after the noise we made at the compound. We were lucky that the clouds had parted and the moon was now bright, bathing our target in clear blue light. I was behind a tree scanning the next hill, looking for any sign of the Patriots in the dark brush. My heart was beating out of my chest and I felt drenched in sweat.

Hugo raised his rifle and took dead aim at Rye, exhaling while pulling the trigger. I heard the crack and saw a little puff at Rye's back. He yelped, and in that instant twisted as he fell, trying to see behind him and grabbing at his back. I can still see that moment as an image in pale blue and jet black shadows. Since anything this traitor said could get hundreds or even thousands of people killed, Hugo fired several shots into Rye until he stopped moving. We knew the suppressors were not enough at this distance, but one could always hope. The only thing we heard after that was silence, then a couple of lonely crickets resumed their song in the distance. Hugo, looking around, silently made his way down the hill toward Rye, searching him for any notes or other intelligence as I kept guard. Finding nothing of value, he pulled off Rye's badges – his name tape, unit patch, dog tags and so on. Throwing them in his pocket, Hugo quietly made his way back up to me and we listened together behind cover.

Chapter 17

Egress

We waited there for minutes, still as stone, until we heard something gently rustling through the brush on the other hill. We knew this was not good, and just as quietly tried to back away from the edge of our hill. We had just gotten off the crest when we heard the sounds get a little more insistent, indicating that whoever it was had picked up speed. As we moved faster, they moved faster. Once we got off the hilltop, we raced downward, then up the next hill, and then down the other side. I was finally able to use the radio to call in an update, along with our location and direction. I let them know we were on the move fast and that Rye had been a traitor but was now dead, along with Lin. I gave them the coordinates of the base, which a US soldier on the other end first identified to our radio operator as Fort Pickett, then corrected himself to Fort Barfoot. To this day, whenever I hear, "Rangers lead the way", I can't help but think – "to what?" This is unfair of course.

At this point Hugo and I could hear shouting, and too many voices for comfort, so we started running again. Once we came to a flat area, we knew we had to make it to the hills on the other side, and then perhaps turn toward the road. If our people could get troops there in time to pick us up, we could avoid a fight. Unfortunately the Patriots were catching up before we could cover the distance to the next hills. Then the firing began. At least the area was heavily forested but as the enemy fired, bits of bark and wood flew off like little pieces of shrapnel. Hugo and I started to fire and retreat – one of us firing back at the Patriots as the other repositioned, and so on, leapfrogging our way back. Just as we had practiced, why not try to hit someone each time, rather than only spending bullets on suppressing fire. We needed every bullet we had. We also used grenades on any of their soldiers who made a rush at us, giving them pause. Those who know what flow is, that is the only way I can describe it. I felt like a machine, like I was acting without acting. I'm not sure how many Patriots and militiamen we managed to shoot in the forest that night but I'm sure when the sun rose there were more than a few dead. We kept the retreat fast and orderly until we had reached the top of the next hill. Here again, time had seemed to stretch out during the fight, and perhaps it was not as wide an expanse as I remember. I do know that with the number of troops shooting at us, it was the forest that had saved us.

Seeing that the terrain was much more in our favor past that hill, Hugo said, "Let's push it!" Our conditioning was almost certainly better than most of the people who were chasing us so this made sense, but it was still completely exhausting. There were a couple of times I got shaky, but Hugo kept me going and gave me some fruit cocktail from a tin that we inhaled in seconds. We avoided the road, running roughly parallel to it. We knew they could simply drive up and shoot us, so we had to outlast them on foot. I was very glad I already had bandages on the backs of my ankles and the balls of my feet, as I usually do.

They had no dogs or ATVs right then, so we just kept running. The night air was cool, and I tried to think of it as an endurance race, keeping pace with Hugo. My muscles were screaming. The further we ran, the closer we got to base, and the more hopeful we got. We'd rest a little, then run some more. The sky was starting to get lighter and we came close to the road. There was no one; the road was empty. We were definitely out of range of small arms fire when we finally saw a small mint green house and red wooden barn, with a white horse fence surrounding the large yard. There was no car there that we could see.

"From lost, to the river! What do you think though?" Hugo said, nodding toward the barn.

"Oh, we're horse thieves now?" I replied.

He just smiled and said, "Wouldn't be the first time!" as he moved to set off down the hill and out of the forest. That's when I noticed he was bleeding, but not from the shot that grazed him earlier. I grabbed him by the shoulder, coaxing him back into cover, and insisted on looking at it. A shot appeared to have grazed the other side of his neck, so I was worried even though it also looked very shallow. He said he felt like he'd also been shot in the back but the armor stopped the bullet, and that hurt worse than the burning from his neck. He must have been the luckiest person I'd ever met. Of course, I also felt a bit guilty because I only had some splinters from the trees, while he'd gotten injured three times. I treated his neck as fast as I could and we set off again with renewed focus.

We made it down to the green house and knocked on the door, but no one answered. We left a hastily written note to the owner, "Tried knocking. Borrowed your horse, will return it - promise". Once we broke into the barn we saw only one horse. We were very fortunate that he seemed to be a good, strong horse; a very dark brown with what appeared to be scarring near his breast and shoulder. I took some time to carefully dress Hugo's wounds, even though when I looked up at him he didn't seem concerned. Then we started to tack up the horse, conscious of the time we were taking. We were able to do this within about fifteen minutes, although it felt like it took forever. I had always been a patient person, even before soldiering, which is why I now wonder if war has had the strange effect of making me less so. Hugo opened the barn door to the morning, and we got ready. He had to take off his pack and strap it to the side of the horse, since I'd ride behind him, wrapping my hands around his waist. He asked me to strap my pack to the other side since it would be too much weight pulling me backward, and we also needed to give the horse a counterweight. We got on the horse, taking a moment to try to reassure the poor thing, and then started off at a good pace. It was hard to say how close behind the Patriots might be, but we didn't want to find out. We also had to be conscious of the weight we were putting on our new friend, and we didn't want him to get exhausted.

Taking the horse onto the 460, Hugo was cautious not to push him to go too fast. We still made good time, but it was a long way back to base. We were careful to ride in the grass to prevent any pain for the horse. To keep ourselves a little more concealed we also kept to the far side of the divided highway. The median provided some cover, and we knew we could head into the woods to hide if necessary. The ride went on for a couple of hours, and there were only two civilian vehicles we saw travelling in the direction of Dinwiddie (which we managed to hide from). We reached a kind of wide crossroads with state route 622 when we saw a pickup truck parked off on the right behind some trees. We heard the rough ignition but kept riding since we knew the driver had seen us. We both kept eye contact with him. I kept my rifle relaxed but ready. It was an older man who rolled his window down, sticking his head out as he approached.

"Y'all need a ride?

"We're ok, thanks", was all Hugo said, eying him. We kept riding in silence.

"You know, there's Patriots in these parts…" the man said as he paced us closely.

153

"I know."

"Listen. You're gonna get yourselves killed" he said, stretching his large weathered hand out the window. "Name's Herold."

"Hugo", he replied, stopping to briefly shake hands.

"Now, if you want a ride somewhere, I can give you a ride. It's a hell of a lot safer than being out here."

Hugo thought for a moment, and looking around said, "Ok, on one condition, I drive".

"Deal" said Herold, opening the door and sliding over to the passenger seat.

We looked at each other in agreement and dismounted. Grabbing our packs, we set the horse loose.

I asked, "How is he going to get back?"

"Horses have built in GPS."

The old man chimed in, "It's true, horses always find their way home. Hop in".

I pulled myself up into the cabin's middle seat, careful to keep my rifle on the left side. "My name is Alba", I said, shaking his hand. Hugo jumped up behind the wheel and swung the door closed. The horse gave us a final look and lowered his head, then turned to take the long walk home.

As soon as we pulled off, Herold reached down near his feet as I watched cautiously. At his feet was a small cooler, from which he pulled a cold can of beer. He popped the top and started drinking. "I was just gonna sit at the crossroads and drink all morning. I needed to get outta the house for once. Folks running around shooting at everything keep me inside most days. Still, this is more excitement than I was expecting." He raised the beer in a salute and finished it off in 30 seconds. Herold held up the empty can in victory and crushed it with one hand, letting it fall to the floor. He bent down to grab another beer, popped the top, and start drinking. For the second time, he drank it down fast.

"Whoa Herold", I said. Without missing a beat, he looked me dead in the eye and crushed the second can in his hand, dropping it on the floor. He bent down for a third beer.

"Harold, is there a good place to pull over in a few minutes?" Hugo asked.

"Sure, there's a few places. Lemme think." He held up the third beer and stared forward, taking a swig. "Why don't you pull off to the right up ahead, there's an old Wal-Mart distribution center" he said, motioning lazily forward.

Hugo said, "I'll just radio in for a vehicle. We can them meet there." Hugo made the call while Harold and I fell quiet. He ended the call with "rapido".

Just as Harold finished the third can, I said, "You know…you can recycle those".

He paused for a moment, gave me that deadpan look again, then crushed the can and released it causing a clank as it hit the other cans on the floor. I couldn't help but laugh. "The distribution center's just up there", he said, nodding ahead and to the right while stooping for another beer. There were already a couple of VAMTACs in the parking lot, waiting for us.

Hugo gave notice over the radio that we were pulling into the lot. We stopped to the left of one of the VAMTACs and nodded to Sebastián, who was seated on the passenger side with his window open. "Herold, thank you. We were lucky you were there. Why don't you wait here for a little while before driving back? Pull around the side and take a nap. We're just going to be talking to our people. Remember, keep this quiet – we weren't here." Herold gave a subtle wink. With that, we got out. Hugo leaned in to leave some cash on the dashboard for gas, and shook Harold's hand.

I leaned over to shake hands as well, saying "Take care of yourself Harold", before making my way over to our vehicles.

As we walked by Sebastián's open window, there was a strong smell of alcohol, but also a kind of chemical smell. "¡Puaj!" I had to sniff my sleeves to make sure Harold hadn't spilled beer on me. Sebastián looked at me, then down. His pupils were dilated and he was sweating. I was shocked. He had been distant, but I couldn't believe he would risk our lives by getting wasted on duty.

Once we got in the back, I leaned over to Hugo and whispered, "Do you smell…?" Hugo had a disappointed look on his face as he looked over at me and nodded. The drive back to Dinwiddie airfield was very quiet. We got back within minutes, and I jumped out quick, waiting to see what would happen. We had pulled up next to the brick and glass airport building, but I am not ashamed to say I pretended to check my pack to see if anything was taken from the night before. I already knew they took my MRE. As I listened to everyone's silent walk to the door, I had one tiny moment of levity. They may have taken my MRE, but I hope they liked squid.

Chapter 18

RETURN

Reaching into the vehicle, Hugo slowly got his gun and pack, waiting for Sebastián to get out. As soon as he did stumble down, Hugo leaned over and said, "Sebastián, I need to talk to you. Follow me". I could feel the tension. They walked into the airport building as I followed at a distance.

Ben was in the other VAMTAC and followed me in. "What's going on Alba? What happened out there? Everyone is so quiet."

"Oh, Ben." I said, putting my hand on his shoulder smugly. "Let's just wait and see. Also, we found a Patriot base and almost got killed, but I'll humbly save that story for another time." We entered the building to see Hugo try a conference room, which was full. The building was actually packed with soldiers, seemingly in every corner. Hugo walked Sebastián into the men's room, followed by "Get out". A bewildered American stumbled out, zipping his fly. What followed is mostly not fit to write, but the whole building fell silent so we could listen. Muffled as the sound was, I could make out every word. I had never heard Hugo yell like that; he was furious, and had every right. It was an excruciating several minutes but no one would have stepped in. Not for a soldier drunk and drugged on duty in a god damned war zone. We need to trust each other too much. I will share how the conversation ended - Hugo yelled that Sebastián would be court-martialed. With that he swung the door open and Hugo stalked outside. We all pretended to already be doing something other than listening. I knew better than to say anything or follow, as did everyone else. He did curtly tell me as he passed that he'd report what happened to us, and to get some sleep. We did our best to return to business as usual, although I'm sure that was no cover. Sebastián opened the door slightly and slunk out of the bathroom red faced, uniform a mess. He looked like he had been crying. He walked outside and that's the last time I saw him. The atmosphere was tense but I needed to rest. After I felt like it wasn't going to become an active shooter situation or total meltdown I nodded off, slumped against the wall. Ben told me later he tried to talk to Sebastián outside but he just said to go away, covering his face. Two from our Civil Guard came to pick him up. I believe he was in fact court-martialed after that and later discharged for bad conduct. Rafael was later brought in from one of our other teams as a replacement, and he was a solid one.

I woke up to Neva kicking my foot. "Alba! You've been asleep for more than 12 hours. Get up!" She kicked my foot again. "You're lucky, Hugo said to let you sleep."

I mumbled something that was supposed to mean, "Fuck! Ok, I'm awake" but it was incoherent noises. When I get a good night's sleep after being awake too long, it always seems like I'm more tired than if I had just stayed up.

That's when I smelled breakfast and jerked up on my feet, grabbing my weapon. Neva laughed at me. The smell was coming from outside but it might as well have been in front of me. My stomach was growling so loud it sounded like it was eating itself. The morning was overcast and drizzling but relatively quiet, which was refreshing. I made my way over to the mess tent, sat down, and ate every morsel with glee. Neva joined me but let me eat without asking anything. Only when we were done, did she ask what happened the day before. I went through the whole story, which she let me finish without interruption. "Fuck. Well that explains it", she said. "There's some kind of major push going on, but no one is saying anything yet. I heard we killed several Patriots a few miles out. I've seen a lot of activity this morning; lots of NATO troops pouring in. We don't have any orders but I'd guess we're preparing to strike that base?"

"Fort Barfoot; yes, that'd be my guess. There's no time to waste, so I'm sure we'll hear soon." With that I suggested we go back in and ask around. On the way out we passed an SAS soldier sitting across from Jessenia. "Jesse! I haven't seen you in too long". Come see us when you finish breakfast." Then I looked at the Brit and said, "Keep your hands above the table". Jessenia giggled at the double meaning, but to show I was (half) serious I pointed two fingers at my eyes, then pointed those fingers at him. "I'm watching you". The soldier just laughed and put his hands up as if to surrender. "Careful."

"-ish" he finished.

We continued out of the mess hall and I asked if anyone had seen Hugo. Miguel told me he was in the conference room and he thought they might be looking for me. I asked who "they" was but he didn't know, other than he saw NATO officers in the conference room. He said there were Canadian soldiers, a British officer, and a couple of Americans. I knocked on the door, and they asked who it was. I was told to wait a few minutes. I could hear a back and forth conversation, but not the content. When they were ready, a soft-spoken American Major opened the door and asked me to take a seat. Hugo was seated toward one end of the table, and I believe eight others took up the rest, tablets at the ready. There were also two soldiers sitting against the wall. I rolled one of the spare seats over to the table, next to Hugo. Without detailing who specifically was in the room, I can verify Spain, Canada, America, Italy, Poland, and the United Kingdom were represented. They asked me to go over the whole story from the previous day. Hugo looked at me and nodded, so I began. I didn't spare any detail, and they asked me to clarify along the way.

After I had finished my story, I thought they were going to ask me to leave. Instead, the American shared the following. Intelligence from multiple sources agreed that General Douglas Hahn was in fact at Fort Barfoot. Even though they seemed to have been pushed back, they defended themselves rather than the territory, inflicting a number of casualties along the way. Hahn was believed to be massing Patriot forces there for a counterattack on our forces around Petersburg, with the ultimate goal of retaking Richmond. They had managed to take the Fort without any warning, and communication had continued as normal. At that moment, it was assumed that any police or military on base were captives. The Navy SEALs had been briefed on this operation, and it was felt (by some) that *they* should ultimately be the ones to capture General Hahn.

I countered that we had been told that was to be our mission. The Major reminded me that the Supreme Allied Commander Europe was American. Of course, SACEUR was always an American. He then changed tack, telling us they had been discussing the operation to capture Hahn with Spain's military leadership, and this had gone all the way up to the King. We had more troops in the area at that time than any other nation individually. With many US soldiers from Virginia tied up in the vicious fight for North Carolina, the numbers spoke for themselves. Hearing of this, the King had insisted on sending even more troops to the region. The Major appeared slightly off put by that outcome, but the US President had already accepted the assistance by phone call. To conclude, he said that he had spoken at length with Carlos (who had at that time been promoted and was still in Richmond) and many others. The whole air of this discussion seemed touchy and political. Apparently, Hugo had stayed up all night talking through a plan by radio with Carlos and many other NATO commanders, who had improved on it. Those in this room and beyond had been further honing the operation all morning. The news that we may have finally found our high value target urgently made its way up the chain. And Hugo had worked to keep the target ours.

As if to make the point, the Major held up a paper, which was a printout of the plan. He passed it down to me, and I tried to absorb it. It was fairly direct – an overwhelming assault on Fort Barfoot, lots of air support, with drone surveillance centered on tracking Hahn. 64 FGNE soldiers, including several junior officers, would capture Hahn alive during the assault. The Navy SEALs would instead capture a UAV company on-site and several other locations on base that might contain the prisoners, as well as valuable intelligence. Any intelligence, especially communications between the Patriots, would help all of us when retaking other areas. Since it was almost certain Hahn would flee under an all out assault on the Fort, the FGNE would have to come in behind enemy lines, roping in from helicopters. This meant the assault would have to be shaped to achieve all military objectives, including retaking the Fort of course, but also driving the direction of retreat. Heavy artillery strikes would reinforce this. Aside from these objectives, killing the enemy was paramount but we were to try to capture equipment with minimal damage wherever possible. Some of the Special Forces groups, which would join regular Spanish forces in the assault, were MOE (our brothers in the Spanish Army), Canadian troops (including CSOR and JTF2), JW GROM and JW Komandosów from Poland, GIS from Italy, and the British SAS. It did not escape my attention that a group from the 75th Ranger Regiment was positioned front and center in this assault, as if to atone for their wayward comrade, Staff Sergeant Rye. Including all US and NATO forces, we had a big numerical advantage. Lastly, the Major announced that leadership was convinced this plan was the best way forward, and that each team would need to be briefed on their portion of the operation. He said not to tell anyone, but that our teams should be ready. We all got ready by sleeping, especially Hugo, who had been up too long.

Meanwhile, NATO troops continued to pour in throughout the next two days, and a sort of tent city was set up to accommodate them all. Planners were very careful to minimize friendly fire by the positioning of forces and segmenting the base accordingly. They used a large augmented reality sandbox to map out Fort Barfoot and the surrounding area. It was literally just a box of sand, but you could push the sand around, and a projector

164

would display an overlay of maps, satellite images, or colorful topographic displays. This was very helpful in visualizing the terrain, troop locations, and enemy installations. We used the most recent satellite images, so although the map is not the territory, it was very close. One could not escape noticing that, in the latest satellite imaging, the Patriots were building up enough forces to counterattack and try to retake Richmond. The Spanish Army would begin the operation by surrounding Fort Barfoot, starting at a distance, in the early morning hours. This investment phase would cut their communications (physically and by electronic attack) when we signaled, and prevent supplies and reinforcements from arriving. Small QRF teams would wait further out from the line of investment and act as circumvallation. Well timed artillery and bombing would then begin to sow confusion and destroy as many of the enemy troops as possible. Targeted munitions were important here, since the Americans wanted to take back as much of the equipment intact as possible. Night would help with that – many of the enemy would be together, asleep, rather than inside of vehicles. Drones and A-10s would target barracks, tents, and certain sectors of the battlefield to avoid friendly fire. After the Air Forces did their job, it was down to the ground forces to clean up. NATO ground forces would be careful to advance steadily during the assault, and prevent the enemy from getting behind them. Since the US had set one of the goals as capturing vehicles and other assets when possible, Special Forces would take up positions to shoot anyone approaching them. Militias, in our experience, could be made to surrender when faced with superior forces. The Patriots, however, would not give up so easy, and might try to destroy everything in the fighting.

Chapter 19

HVT

Two days later, each team was briefed on the mission, and their parts in it. We also had a larger gathering of the special forces for a final mission brief where we introduced ourselves, one team at a time, to avoid friendly fire. I made sure to remember each face. At twilight, Spanish forces set out to surround the Fort at a distance, which was a very large effort in itself. A light drizzle rained down, as though protecting our side. Since everyone had networked white phosphorous night vision goggle binoculars running the augmented reality Combat Cloud, we were able to easily gather information and classify the enemy troops, equipment, and positions. Several small observation cameras were also set at certain vantage points to provide CC with continuous coverage. All of this coverage was mixed with existing satellite data. Viewed through the goggles, the enemy was silhouetted like a line drawing (or highlighted if desired), and controls, which allowed for labeling objects, included tagging individuals. Speech to text for the labels combined with voice commands, which meant that the soldier didn't even have to remove their finger from the trigger. For instance, (if you were feeling spicy) you could label an individual "Red shirt backwards cap LMG asshole", or "Patriot Commander". You could highlight any individual with various colors, so there was nowhere they could run on the battlefield that the system wouldn't track them. CC used gait recognition, facial recognition, and a number of other classified identifiers to track people who get tagged. Everyone using CC can see all of this. The color could even be labeled (for the colorblind). There was actually a standardized coding system to labeling people, places, things, and actions that I won't disclose. That enabled coherent data dumps (for later analysis) of what worked, tactically, and what didn't. The network of satellite, drone, fighter jets, optics, and so on, all melded into an AI driven system of systems: this was our combat cloud, or CC as we called it in America. In Spanish we would say Nimbocombate. To those familiar with video games, this was a huge advantage, and was not the fully realized soldier's reality until the second American war. All the data fed back to base too, with information about their troops and ours. Obviously, this is like a tactical superpower, and allowed for more accurate planning.

The Spanish Army reported that they were in place, and keeping their distance. They reported that a surveillance drone had to be neutralized by EW. No other EW action was taken at that time. Comms were intercepted showing that the Patriots believed the problem came from drone control malfunction. Militia patrols reported nothing unusual. Our own surveillance was in place.

Civilians who lived near the front line were temporarily detained and guarded by Spanish troops to prevent them from notifying anyone. I'm sure they hated that and felt violated, but some of them would have felt no compunction about making a phone call and getting thousands of people killed in the service of their authoritarian cult. The consequences of their choices were unavoidable. Some NATO Special Forces teams then infiltrated a staging area near the fort using stealthy helicopters. Everyone was looking out for Hahn, and we were lucky that one of our soldiers was able to tag him using CC. Later that night, the aerial bombardment of Fort Barfoot began. Several F-35s and bombers used highly targeted munitions to decimate large masses of Patriots in their barracks. Wherever the enemy were already inside vehicles, those had to be destroyed by drones and Super A-10s for our own safety, which prevented any hope of counterattack. The timing and location of fire was designed to make Hahn flee through the one free and unopposed section of the base. In fact, that "free" section was an enlarged gauntlet, with the Spanish army waiting at a distance. The gauntlet was like an open thumb on a mitten, with soldiers concealed and hidden behind cover to prevent friendly fire. There would be no escape this time. Since Hahn did not know he had been tagged, or even our exact capabilities, he was unaware of the trap.

I remember that night was muggy and uncomfortable. Our 64-person FGNE team had already geared up and jumped onto the helos, ready for what we hoped would be our decisive moment. The Night Stalkers from the US 160th were carrying the Navy SEALs, and we all awaited the signal. I had wondered why Delta Force had to sit this one out, but I found out later it was due to the heavy enemy activity around Fort Liberty. One of the SEALs looked at us and touched his helmet, and we returned the gesture. The order was given, and our helicopters lifted in quick succession, like dragonflies from a log. Looking out the window of the helicopter, I saw no lights on the ground to speak of. The power was out, as in many areas, so the darkness simply passed below to the quiet sound of the rotors. On approach, our groups spilt up, with the Night Stalkers pulling away for their portion of the mission. We arrived just outside Fort Barfoot in about 12 minutes and fast roped to the ground. We were told that it appeared Hahn would probably be hustled into his JLTV soon, so we took up positions. Our team set up snipers if needed. Many others were concealed among the pines, or behind shallow hills for defilade.

Hahn had tried to run in one of three JLTVs, which they must have thought would confuse us. The three vehicles tried to turn South off Military Rd., then split up, one of them taking a worn old road called Mosby. The vehicles were disabled before they could gain distance from each other by using Carl Gustavs with small cartridges and high powered sniper rifles. This forced all of the occupants to stumble out concussed, or at least dazed. It was dawn now and we could see them against the hazy pink which was edging out the blue of the early morning sky. There were twelve of the enemy in all and we quickly closed distance to detain them. Hugo held his pistol on Hahn, and asked me to grab any intel from the passenger side of the vehicle.

The battle seemed to be nearing us. I heard Hugo yelling over the sound of gunfire: "General Hahn! Show me your hands! Turn away from me! Hands on your head! Lace your fingers! Slowly walk backwards toward me! Get on your knees! *Get on your fucking knees*! Cross your feet!" Hugo reached from behind, grabbed Hahn's fingers, and stepped over his crossed feet. Just as he had slung his gun back down and disarmed Hahn, we heard the sudden crack of bullets whizzing by, and many of the detainees who still had them went for their side arms. At close quarters, two of our soldiers were shot, sustaining minor injuries. Using his knee, Hugo shoved Hahn face down. I returned fire too, coming back round the corner of the vehicle. Hugo made a call for immediate close air support to suppress the enemy closing in on us. I heard him arguing with a pilot, "danger close, send in". There were a few tense minutes where all we could do was return fire. An A-10 strafed the enemy, followed by two attack helicopters. The pace of gunfire seemed to slow down. We felt safe enough to start to move the prisoners. I saw Hugo reach down to pick Hahn up off the ground, when a shot from beyond the trees struck Hugo in the cheek. He slowly turned, took a step forward, and fell down. Hahn looked around, wild eyed, then jumped to his feet and bolted for the pines. Miguel leapt over to Hugo and immediately started to provide first aid.

I must have been in shock, because I *knew* Hugo was fine, and if anyone would survive it was going to be him. As I watched Hahn run into the brush, my only feeling in that moment was pure rage. I ran after him at top speed, along with a few fellow soldiers flanking to my left and right. They lay down suppressing fire in the direction of the gunshots to keep the enemy's heads down. Hahn had just enough of a head start, and just enough cover to conceal him for a short while. I yelled out to surround the small patch of forest. Utility roads encircled it, and he would not be leaving that place a free man. I kept low and stalked into the forest toward where I knew he was. He had freed his hands and tried to ambush me from behind the undergrowth, but I side kicked his knee and smashed the barrel of my gun into his nose as he went down. Blood squirted out and trickled down his face as he fell backward, but he rolled along the ground and actually came back up.

Raising his hand to his face, he felt his nose and tried to wipe away some of the blood. His face was wild, unfocused. He reached down to his hip and pulled out a combat knife, yelling, "Come on!

I'll die a free man." With that he furiously signaled to come closer. I didn't argue; I didn't say a word.

I remembered the Destreza teacher we could never touch. I remembered how fast and agile he was with his sword, always several steps ahead. But it was his stillness at the beginning that let us know we would never win. My heart would always sink a little when facing him, knowing that no matter how much I trained, I could only lose well. This is the benefit of exemplars in our lives. Hahn was a trained soldier and a leader, but I had faced people I knew I could never surpass, and he was not one of them. I didn't hesitate. At first glaring at him from behind my HK, I smoothly lowered the gun, stepping back with my left foot. It was like the world became silent. I could hear the soft crush of leaves on the ground as I moved without error. I relaxed and stood tall, my shoulders easing back fully. Just as smoothly, I brought my right hand over to my left breast for the knife Hugo had given me. I drew it from the sheath slowly, easily, and with certainty. All the while I kept commanding eye contact but said nothing. I slowly lowered the knife to float over my right thigh. As I stepped forward lightly on my right, my left foot shifted to the side, and my right shoulder followed.

I stared at him, completely relaxed, and completely motionless. The dappled light danced across his face, covering his green eyes with shade. What he must have seen in my own eyes was murder. There was yelling and gunfire in the distance, and my team was closing in, but I'm certain all that Hahn and I could hear was the silence. Passive resignation crept into his eyes before he lowered them. Then like snow, which falls from the branches of an evergreen on a still winter's day, the knife slipped from his hand, sticking point first into the Virginia ground. General Hahn slumped to his knees and put his hands on his head. I put him face down and handcuffed him as my soldiers were closing in.

"Douglas Hahn, by the principle of universal jurisdiction, you are under arrest for the murder of Spanish citizens, for war crimes, and for crimes against humanity." He said nothing as we walked him back out of the woods, and would not make eye contact. The sun was up and the sky was mostly clear. The day was getting hot. The kind of hot that prickles the skin, makes you irritated. Someone had already called the helicopters in for exfil, and to take the wounded. I saw Hugo loaded on a stretcher in one of them. Miguel and Rafael took Hahn and brought him onto one of the other Chinooks. I ran over to see about Hugo, but that's when I saw it was bad, and my heart sank. I got close enough to touch his neck, just for a moment. The medic pushed me away, to which I could only say, "Please, take care of him".

Chapter 20

DESOLATION

They were pulling many of us up into the helicopters, but I hesitated to sit down. Hahn, already strapped in, looked at me, then at Hugo, then back at me, and he *smiled.* It was the grisly smile of someone with poison in their heart. Time seemed to slow down. There was heavy gunfire still going on. I felt deep sadness, anger, and indecision creeping in. My eyes started to tear up, because I wanted to shoot him but couldn't. Then everything lensed into perfect clarity. I took two steps back, and yelled out that I wasn't coming. I was going back to join the battle. One of the helicopter crew yelled back, "Are you fucking crazy?" but I just kept stepping backward.

Then I stopped to look at everyone and yelled out, as loud and sharp as I could, "¡Viva España!"

Everyone in earshot yelled back just as sharply, *"¡Viva!*

Miguel nodded to me, he understood. After yelling something to the medics, he was the first to jump back out. His boots hit the ground with a satisfying thud. Then I saw Neva, Ben, Jesse, and Rafael jump out, and many others followed. I think most of us, except those guarding Hahn and the injured, ended up staying. With that the helicopters were breaking station, returning to base. There was no objective now but to lay hate and waste on these so-called Patriots; traitors to their own people and a scourge to everyone. I thought it then and have no regret in repeating it now, *fuck them*. Fuck their cruelty, fuck their smug ignorance, fuck their absurd lies, fuck their dishonor. *Fuck them*.

When I said we laid waste to them, I meant it. I was yelling for everyone, even though I wasn't in charge. The more I yelled, the more rage I felt. We called for any free Pizarros, Dragons, Leopards and VAMTACS to come around. Our brothers and sisters in MOE showed up in minutes. I remember yelling that if the enemy didn't surrender to waste them. We all knew the rules of engagement, but I was trying to influence the *tone*. If they didn't drop their gun standing up, they could do it crumpled on the ground in a pool of their own blood. We would not do anything illegal, and they should be glad for it. The rage was visceral, and I had no mercy left, only obligations. In that moment I wished we could use Molotov cocktails to clear every building and just burn them all alive. It would have been so satisfying to shoot them as they spilled out of doorways and windows, screaming and in flames. I would have gladly traded my HK for a flamethrower if they were still legal. I wanted to burn away the lies with fire. I could have beaten them to death with a rock, or cut them down with a sword. But I wouldn't betray my obligation to the military code. Short of that, the Patriots were about to reap what they had sown. Each one of us was energized; all of our training was set free with no orders but victory. We became shock troops.

Miguel took full command of our group at that point. Using CC to locate the enemy, we headed toward the nearest buildings, the first of which was the Officer's Club, where we could see heavy activity. A number of our vehicles began to surround the Club, and also the nearby gym building. Miguel called out by loudspeaker to surrender immediately and come outside. The response was that the enemy open up on us from nearly every window, and some shots also came from the gym. We lit them the fuck up. Every vehicle opened fire, then we pulled back, calling in air support. One of our Tiger attack helicopters fired a couple of missiles, one into each building. Huge explosions ripped through the structures, and the sound was almost deafening, but cheers went up from all of us. A few of the enemy continued to fire from the Club; I'm not even sure how anyone survived. We used CC and our optics to target the holdouts more accurately. Then we advanced on the remainder since they wouldn't give up, killing all of them. We started to fan out to clear the entire base. The armies were all doing their job in the other sectors, based on the radio comms. The SEAL teams had managed to save nearly all of the vehicles in the north lots, although several tanks and APCs were missing. They were probably the ones we had taken out by air, artillery, and anti-tank missile. We were preventing any escape to the South. NATO Special Forces groups, and the Spanish Army, were assaulting Patriot strong points wherever they found them.

Inside the remains of the gym, I thought we had cleared a narrow workout corridor with various workout machines. As I foolishly doubled back alone, on a feeling, I came by a shallow recess. A man, who had somehow perched himself on the top of a weight machine there, shot once with a pistol (which missed) and then leapt down at me. With his left hand, he tried to grab my rifle in midair while pointing the pistol toward my head. I reacted in a blink, leaning back and slapping the back of my hand against his wrist, then grabbing it firmly. He fired again just as I gained control. I drove my left elbow under his bicep hard, locking his arm. Pulling his gun hand past me, I twisted. Shifting my left arm to apply downward pressure, his body doubled over just as he tried to grab at my rifle again with his free hand. Slipping my left hand up, I pulled my knife out in an icepick grip, and stabbed him in the temple as hard as I could. His knees buckled, but I freed the knife and stabbed into the side of his neck as his eyes dimmed. I sawed upward, in and out, like a butcher cutting meat at an odd angle. Blood sprayed everywhere, but I completed cutting as he sunk onto the ground. Blood pooled quickly on the mats as I stood upright, an electric feeling coursing through me, a sick surreal euphoria. Blood soaked into my uniform, and it had spattered on my face. I pulled down my neck gaiter to wipe off my face, but then my lips tasted like salty copper. I cleaned the blade on my thigh and sheathed it.

Looking back, surely it was necessary to defend myself with the knife? A naïve psychologist might have something to say about control or transference, but I thought: No. I've seen enough. They have raped and murdered and tortured the innocent. They have hurt people I know. Now they need to give in, or else be destroyed.

I yelled "Clear!", in case anyone heard, then made my way back out telling no one. Neva tried to check me for injuries, but I only told her it wasn't my blood as I passed. For the rest of the assault I made sure to stay with the others. As the morning wore on, the day became overcast. We encountered minor resistance from both the fire and emergency services buildings, so four teams went into each and cleared them. We came across barracks, which had already been struck, but once again we were being fired upon. There we stayed back to call in the American's A-10s for a couple passes. This was highly effective and many of the Patriots tried to run, but we opened fire on them, killing many. The sound of my rifle filled my ears, crack, crack, crack, followed by the report echoing out over the pavement, and the brass plinking on the ground. Any who fled too far would be met by the regular army and killed or captured. There was what appeared to be two suicide drones released from the barracks, which we destroyed using the grenade launchers on our vehicles to fire airbursts. Then we turned those same automated grenade launchers on the barracks themselves. To be clear, the kinds of grenades we used could fire in quick succession and explode in cones of shrapnel, piercing walls. Shrapnel and fragments from the wall would shred anyone standing in that area. We also called in another salvo of artillery. After that, we could hear no movement left in the buildings. As we cleared what was left of each building, finding only the dead, it seemed to me that more people should have surrendered than did, but they really must have believed they were right.

We saw the Patriots had already started to dig trenches throughout the base, an effort that was incomplete. Many trenches were empty. Still, the enemy did manage to take out a couple of our vehicles using TOW missiles, and a number of casualties ensued. At least one loitering munition completely destroyed a VAMTAC, killing several. We took the enemy's tenacity and lack of surrender as signing their own death warrant. We would run or drive, positioning ourselves in quick L-shaped assaults, or advance with bounding over watch. We so outnumbered them that sometimes we simply sprinted at them using cover. CC made it very easy to catch the enemy from two sides while having excellent situational awareness of their movements. Our soldiers would try to fire at the right time, from the right position, and with such overwhelming numbers, as well as having air support, that it was amazing the Patriots continued to resist as long as they did. When they tried to retreat, we would cut as many down as we could, then close in with grenades and small arms, making sure no one lived who did not surrender. And not enough surrendered to us. The regular army took the majority of the prisoners. Given the number of the dead, there is one thing I would say about Spain's military forces throughout history: we may seem relentless, but when we see we are wrong, we do relent in the end. In this case, we were not wrong.

Currents of black smoke lifted from every part of the base, choking the morning air. Popping sounds could be heard in the buildings, then the rush and crackle of fires. The smell was acrid: the sulfur odor of hair, the charcoal smell of burnt flesh - the look of it is like bits of charred beef jerky. Over this was the toxic smell of artificial materials, with overwhelming notes of plywood, burnt rubber, carpet, and the sugary smell of burning insulation. Bodies and parts of bodies were everywhere. Some had their faces peeled back, some were missing limbs, many looked like they were sleeping soundly. There must have been more than two thousand of them. The concrete and brick was pocked everywhere from grenades and bullets, while broken glass and bits of wood were scattered across the ground. Some buildings caught fire completely, which engulfed several structures, but we let them burn. By late afternoon the operation was mostly complete. Once we had made certain that all resistance was neutralized, we asked for exfil by our helos, which arrived in less than fifteen minutes. As we hopped in the helicopters I stayed quiet. Ben yelled something like "I'm sure Hugo is fine." Miguel just gave me a look as if to say, "You don't have to answer." As we pulled up and away, the base was in ruins. The smoke had gotten thicker, and our Military Emergencies Unit was finally beginning to control the fires. In the sky, I was glad to be clear of it all, but felt emotionless, thoughtless. This must be what purgatory feels like, if there was one.

I remember wishing that I had been driven back, which would have given me more time. One thing that helped me was the cool wind and the light drizzle. It let me know I was still alive. The dread of landing back at Dinwiddie was awful, because I didn't know what had happened to Hugo. When I landed, there were a couple of Americans who wanted to talk about getting everyone together for debriefs. To one I vacantly said, "They're gone". He asked who was gone, and I repeated impatiently while looking past him, "They're gone. The Patriots. They're gone." Then I asked one US medic where surgery would be and he pointed me to a series of medical tents that were the combat support hospital. I turned and jogged past the scrum of soldiers into the tents.

On entering the first tent a medic stopped me, seeing my state, but I asked him if he knew where Hugo was. He said "Come talk to me outside" and tried to gently touch my arm. I withdrew my arm, twisting to slip right by him through a corridor leading to the next tent. I heard him yell after me, but I assumed he was only trying to divert me. I nearly bumped into another medic in an adjoining tent. I saw medical equipment and beds but only two men I didn't know lay in them. The two medics gently herded me out. I asked again if they knew whether Hugo had been there. They said that he had been.

The first medic I had run into looked at me sadly and tried to put his hand on my arm again. I gently used the edge of my palm to block his wrist and push it away. "Say it."

"He's gone. I'm sorry", the medic said.

That's all I needed to hear. I nodded and stalked out of the tent with a pressure building behind my eyes and around my head. Outside, I tried to kneel on the dark, wet asphalt, feeling nauseous, my head pounding. I couldn't throw up. I couldn't cry. I even took my helmet off and tried lying on the rain-soaked ground. After a few minutes, I stood up and went back into the tent. I thought about asking the young medic for something to help me sleep. I reconsidered when I realized it could be disqualifying, and I was not remotely thinking about ending my service. It was my duty, and I couldn't abandon. Instead, I asked if his body was still there, and whether I could see him. Even that was not possible, they told me, as he had already been flown back to Dover AFB with many others. No release, no sleep, no pill, no closure. Nothing. And anyway, Plus Ultra. There is no way forward but forward I told myself.

I slowly returned to where I had last seen my group, only to find soldiers scattered everywhere. It was now a tangled mess of troops from many countries which, once entered, was hard to exit. There was awful jubilation among the crowd which I didn't want to be near, it was suffocating. I finally found Miguel and asked him where I needed to be. He and the others must have just come from seeing about Hugo themselves. He walked me over to the others, who were consoling each other when I came up. Neva gave me a big hug, which I politely accepted. I protested that I was ok, and that Hugo lost his life in battle, so glory was his. No doubt they heard my voice waver and crack, which made Neva tear up. I asked Miguel if there was anything else, but he softly told me there was nothing left to do.

Chapter 21

REPRISALS

After sleeping like a stone that night, I was up early the next morning. Breakfast was very rich, with everyone still in a victorious mood. I ate like a raven and left in minutes. I heard that we had no notice about the takeover at Fort Barfoot because many of the communications people were loyal to the Patriots. Everyone loyal was killed. It was another example of heavy infiltration leading to loss. The dead included civilians, soldiers, US Marshals, ATF, FBI, and Virginia State Police. I am told the State Police put up a particularly hard fight (based on their injuries), but their radio systems had been sabotaged and cell service silenced in the area. The Patriots themselves were often known to use bike messengers to keep their own comms private. Most of the deceased were unceremoniously thrown in mass graves on the property. Bulldozers hadn't even finished putting all the bodies in the ground when we arrived. Many of their hands were bound behind their back before they were killed and some showed signs of torture. The US Army was there for the next few days exhuming all those who remained loyal to the end, and taking away the remains of the traitors we had left on the ground. Attempts were always made to see if relatives might claim the body, and many did. An American told me that several videos were found on the phones of dead Patriots showing the torture, and some of the last troopers were murdered in horrible ways. He said when he heard the first sounds on one of the beheading videos, he immediately shut it off. The troopers did not give up any useful information in those videos and lost no honor. Why is it that those who proclaim the greatest purity are often the same ones making snuff films? There were other videos which were purely for propaganda, similar to those we saw on social media. They proclaimed a new United States of America and other self-serving garbage. We thought, given their setbacks the Patriots might counterattack to retake Richmond, or even attack the Americans at Fort Gregg-Adams, but instead they took Fort Barfoot without us hearing of it. Hahn had often been very crafty, but he had also forgotten the cardinal rule of guerrilla war: move among the people. Massing a large part of his forces must have been due to overestimating his own capabilities, or underestimating everyone else. I suspect it was the latter.

The next day, however, the enemy did try to prove they could reappear at will. At our own base, we suddenly came under sustained fire by mortars, and at least one big Howitzer, all from the North. As we kept under cover, a truck bomb detonated at the fence, sending up a massive blast. A large number of local militia and Patriots tried a quick charge while we were under fire, followed by a retreat. They repeated this tactic several times, perhaps hoping to get inside our lines. This wasn't completely ineffective, since we took several casualties from shelling, while the enemy boldly advanced. There were too many of us for the enemy to have ever hoped they could win, but I suppose it was meant as a message. Our protection forces did an excellent job. We also responded once it was safe to, and picked off some of those who struggled to escape in time. After we saw how determined they were, we knew that we'd have to annihilate them, but just as quickly they retreated from the area. Something about their attack, as well as their sudden retreat, seemed a little too perfectly timed and coordinated.

With all the intrigue around military moles, someone had the insight to talk to the Americans about their access to CC. The combat cloud was like a secret weapon, but a double-edged sword. Since the US demanded to be in the loop on everything, even against our advice, their access to the combat cloud might compromise operations. The Patriots were seemingly embedded everywhere. We even spoke with Tim from the CIA, who directed us to a DoD contact. Without relaying all the details, there was a kind of API for the combat cloud that we had set up for the Americans to use our data so they could blend it with their own systems. Patriots were still hiding throughout the US military, and had sympathizers among the families and friends of active duty members and veterans alike. This event was yet another reminder.

It turned out that someone had been querying the system and giving intel to the Patriots. The mole was a woman named Emma Novak, an information technology specialist. The Americans put her to death the following year for treason. She had a lover who had joined the Patriots, he was her reason. Quite simply, the Patriots wanted revenge on us. After the attack on our base, we let the Americans know that we could no longer allow them direct access to CC, for their protection and ours. They were not happy, seemingly valuing information over lives, but we held our ground. There would simply be too many losses doing it their way, so we kept an air gap on certain intelligence. We summarized everything truthfully for them, but kept the raw data to ourselves. Instead, we scrubbed everything and timed the release of information to draw out moles. We apologized to the Americans, but security was paramount.

I must mention that immediately following the assault on Fort Barfoot, and perhaps as retribution, Fort Liberty in North Carolina had also come under more frequent but still minor attacks. The Patriots and those militias throughout the Deep South were not using the same violence of action during this time as those we encountered in Virginia. The hope was that they were either receding in popularity, or cowed by harsh losses in Virginia. Either way, the Americans were taking a softly, softly approach throughout the South. The uptick in activity was worrying, since attacking Fort

Liberty seemed suicidal. It is a truly giant installation, at about six hundred fifty square kilometers and well over fifty thousand military personnel. It was one of the main bases for projecting force on the East coast, especially toward the South. For a while we ignored these minor incursions, but I remember thinking, even then, that the enemy was testing the US defenses from the inside and out; probing for weakness. It was a clever strategy.

The Army started to get reports of kamikaze drone attacks against Fort Liberty's generators, radar, comms, followed by loss of some communication. A saturation attack by EMPs came next, likely using a couple types of E-bombs, probably low frequency FCG and vircators. The microwave bombs crippled functionality in parts of the base. At the time it was thought these may have been mounted in cruise missiles, but it turned out to have been GPS guided glide-bombs from a distant bomber that was ditched shortly after, crashing into a field. The pilot was never found, because of course. The part that worried people is, not only was it highly effective, but the bombs were not part of inventory (one dud was found), and must have been purpose built. This was not the work of one treasonous pilot. The bombing was combined and coordinated with terrorist attacks to take out electrical power, with fire and explosives being used on electric poles and substations in and around the base.

Military families living in towns off base had been marked in Aberdeen, Raeford, Lillington, Sanford, Hope Mills, Pinehurst, Southern Pines, Whispering Pines, Vass, and even Fayetteville. The Patriots had local informants mark the front doors of each home during the night with red paint, a reversal of the story of exodus. If you had the mark, you were killed. Small fire teams were sent that night to liquidate the entire family and anyone else who was in the home. Although the Patriot fire teams met with strong resistance, losing some of their men, in the end far too many of the off-base military families were killed. The rest managed to flee to base, where the situation finally stabilized.

Following that sad night, likely Patriot informants started to be killed in retribution. A large number of their homes were hit by Molotov cocktails, burning not only the possible traitors, but their whole families alive. Civil Wars are particularly brutal affairs, and it did not surprise me when the culprits for these fires were never arrested by the police. One who is never looked for cannot be found. Just as suddenly as the attacks on Fort Liberty had commenced, they ceased. The military was then sequestered on base for safety. However, in this way the remaining traitors could move more freely among the people.

I suppose I should mention that not long after we retook Fort Barfoot, I received a congratulatory call from Carlos himself, who had become quite a big shot. Many had already been calling him Che, but I stopped using that nickname due to his rank. He said that he would be recommending me for the Laureate Cross of Saint Ferdinand, for capturing General Hahn. I couldn't think of what to say for a moment. I wasn't sure I deserved it. He even asked if I was still on the line. I said "Thank you sir, it's an honor", and rushed to get off the line as soon as I could. There was no way I could think about any of that for long. Not at that time.

Chapter 22

DREAM

Rather than our Special Forces groups going out on patrols, which the army was already doing, we were frequently sent into areas with a heavy militia and Patriot presence to complete kill or capture missions. If they were on our list, or tried to kill us, we could engage. If they were in a known enemy militia, or a member of the Patriots, we could engage if they did not comply. We had set up many sensors and small drones to advise us of anyone in the area, especially after the sudden attack after our own assault on Fort Barfoot. The enemy grew smaller in number.

One day we were waiting for a group of militia members to cross a wetland in a former conservation area north of base. I think the fact that the area was wetland gave the enemy a false sense of security, especially because it was raining that day. Little did they know, in the 16th century, there was a sailor by the name of Pedro Menéndez de Avilés who was a scourge of pirates, and later, the founder of Saint Augustine in Florida. In 1565, the French tried to crush the new Spanish settlement with a fleet under Jean Ribault. A heavy storm tore through the region. The French were sheltering in Fort Caroline, which was under the command of René Goulaine de Laudonnière. Menéndez marched his men through the swamps for two days, in the middle of a hurricane, to attack Fort Caroline at dawn. Menéndez put them all to the sword and returned to Saint Augustine. After the storm, the French fleet under Ribault had been shipwrecked, so Menéndez doubled back and caught several hundred of the French who were marching north. In a shameful episode, he also put them to the sword, even after they had given up. My point is, if the militia thought a little rain and some underbrush were going to prevent Spanish soldiers from clearing the area, they must never have learned the history of the Americas.

This seemed to be one of the enemy's standard patrols, but they had also tried reconnaissance near our base before. Sometimes there was sniper fire from the North. It was clear that we needed to clear this small group out. We now camouflaged ourselves with local brush and grasses, until we resembled the grounds. We were spread out, but I was situated between Neva and Ben. The militia in question had helped to kill many of the citizens in Petersburg and after we took the city, they had fled to the local wilderness. We saw a few of the mortars and a small encampment, very sparse yet very mobile. Most of the time the militia stayed on the wooden bridges and paths, but as I was waiting in the bushes, one of the men separated from the group and approached. Moving off to the side of a short natural path of low grass between higher growth and water, I waited to create a possible ambush. I could hear the rest of his patrol moving further away, all the while talking to each other loudly. This man had a goatee and curved sunglasses with a bucket hat. It seemed like he was going to take a piss but since he was practically on top of me, and with his back to me, I reacted. He was unzipping his pants just as I guessed. I silently drew my knife and slowly rose up. I felt when he started to sense my presence, and didn't want to alert his group. Just as his head started to turn I covered his mouth and stabbed deep into his neck, pulling out to sever the windpipe. I finished him off by stabbing him in the heart and kidneys. Then we rolled him off the path behind the tall grass, and dragged his body into some muddy swamp water. This wasn't perfect because now the grass was disturbed. I moved further away for concealment, and partially submerged myself into the mud.

One of the other militia members called out to the man with the goatee, once, a pause, twice. I didn't make a sound. As I heard the man backtracking along the path, I knew he would step off into the short grass to follow his friend. I was already using the cover of the tall grass and water to move around to the side of where he'd end up, ready to make my way out behind him on the path. It was a natural trap. The second man made his way over. A short, jolly looking fellow, he had a big middle aged belly but a thin beard like a teenager. As they say, each soldier fights for their comrades, so I knew he would investigate. He walked slowly, following the disturbed grass, raised his AR-15, and began to lean forward. The rain helped to soften the sound of my advance. I slowly drifted close to him with my rifle focused on the back of his head. Just as I thought, he inched closer and leaned over the tall grass, trying to see beyond. Despite the hard stares of my comrades I lowered my rifle and drew my knife. Enveloping his neck with my left forearm, I jerked his head to the side and cut deeply across the throat, twice. His right hand left the rifle's trigger as I felt it would, reaching for his neck. I was able to slow his fall, rolling him into the reeds. Ben then pulled him behind the grass into the water. We crawled out of the brush and wetlands, making our way toward the camp.

At this point, the other militiamen had put some distance between them and us. With no one left guarding the camp, we advanced to take a look. It's quite possible the two men I killed were supposed to be standing guard. We circled the clearing from the tree line and, seeing nothing of value but a couple of mortars, took up positions on two sides of the camp. We waited for a short time before planting explosives and destroying all their equipment plus the weapons they had left behind. Then we waited for everyone to come running. The militia tried to use cover to approach but saw their camp had been destroyed. We had retreated to better ground, ready for an ambush if necessary. Miguel called out to them, "Surrender! Place your weapons above your heads and come out."

A voice called out from the bushes, "who are you?"

Miguel called back, "We're Spanish soldiers. We outnumber you and we have the high ground. There's no need to fight."

They seemed to whisper to themselves, when one of them yelled, "Fuck that!"

As expected, they did not surrender. Gunfire opened up on us from the bushes, first one gun, then several. We had marked their locations and picked them off, except for one. There were five of them we had shot but one surrendered, a teen with a dirty face and scruffy hair. He yelled, "wait, wait!" clearly terrified. The boy approached unarmed, hands up, so we took him into custody and talked to him further as we drove back. He said that he had fallen in with the group a short while before because his parents had been killed and he had nowhere else to go. They told him that America was being invaded and that's what the war was really about. That's why they were shelling our base. When we showed up, he almost believed the invasion story, but in the end he didn't want to die. We explained that ours was not an invasion force but that we had been invited into the US due to the ongoing civil war. Our role was to help resolve the conflict.

He asked a good question, which was, "How could I know whose side to take?" I didn't answer, but I was listening. "I was all alone. The world is hard now. The only way I was gonna survive was to become a hard man. Right?" I had to think about that for a moment.

I stared ahead as we jostled around in the back of the truck, then turned to look him in the eyes. "No. That isn't the way. We make the world hard, but it gets easier with understanding."

When we finally got back to base, we turned the young man over. I smelled like a swamp. Miguel unexpectedly asked to talk with me. We went in a room, and he shut the door. He seemed let down, saying, "Alba, I need to know that you're ok."

"I don't know a potato about why I wouldn't be. What do you mean?"

"Other than a couple of stories, every soldier I have ever served with who made it to retirement did so without using a knife to kill."

"Hold on..."

"Let me finish. What you did was legal, I'm not saying it wasn't, but Neva told me that you nearly cut some guy's head off at Fort Barfoot. So I'm worried about you."

"Fucking Neva"

"Don't blame her, she doubled back. I can see it on your face. If we were weaker people we wouldn't say a thing, we'd let it go. But I think maybe you need to talk with someone."

"Miguel..."

"Relax, I don't mean it has to be official, but I see you're hurting. You can talk to me, or Neva, or any of us. About...anything", he said knowingly.

"You know that right? And please, do me a favor, I want you to start writing down your thoughts, that's what helps me. Or paint, or something like that. You can't carry all of this weight around, it'll break you. You know I only say this as a friend. We care about you, and we want to help. Ok?"

"Fine, Miguel."

"Ok, that's all I ask. Now, get cleaned up, get some food, and get some rest."

I am not often comfortable sharing personal things, so perhaps it's strange that I should choose to share the following dream, but I have my reasons. I don't usually remember my dreams, so what I will relate is also a rarity. I remember being asleep in the passenger side of an older model car when I woke up with a start. I felt no fear, no anxiety, and no exhaustion. The car's interior was painted in glossy cream with red and black leather seats. There was a sort of awareness that I might be dreaming but it felt so *real*. I felt the leather seat, smooth on my hands, and I could even hear the texture as my fingers slid across. The air had a slight chill, and I had a nice outfit on with a light three-quarter-length jacket. Maybe it was spring, perhaps some future morning. It was strange because I couldn't see out of the windows. It took me a moment to realize it was fog or condensation, but I could also see warm sunlight illuminating the clean interior. There was a faint melody starting to play that I couldn't recall, something melancholy. I checked the radio but it was off, in fact there were no keys in the ignition. As my mind cleared, I realized that it was Hugo's old Seat 600, but fully restored. I traced my finger down the cool condensation, creating a sliver of clarity; a little window on a sunny morning. Then a sudden tap on the car window startled me. I slid over to the other side and opened the door. The morning was sunny and damp, and I couldn't place the location, but I think maybe it was the rose garden in Parque del Buen Retiro. As I stepped out it was so resplendent, so green, and beyond a wrought iron gate there were bright roses and other flowers tumbling over each other to catch the eye with their dewy glow. Standing there was Hugo, sharply dressed in layers - a nice shirt and tie, a brown jacket, and jeans. I wanted to say something but he smiled first and raised a paper coffee cup with a black lid, one of two. I took it. It was warm against my cold hands and it smelled rich. Instead of saying anything I suddenly leaned in and hugged him, my wrist and cup resting against his neck, his cheek against mine. My hair was down for once. He brushed it back with his finger and, resting his hand on my cheek, our lips met. I kept my eyes open the whole time, afraid to shut them. Then he nodded toward the park and offered his arm. I took it and we walked down the avenue. I started to feel a sort of out of body experience. Floating silently into the air, I could see us walking and laughing under the shade of emerald leaves in the cool of an early morning. As I floated even higher than the treetops I saw myself resting my head on his shoulder, and then I woke up in confusion.

I wasn't sure if this was now a dream within a dream, but I could feel tears running down my face, and my sleeping bag was wet beneath my cheek. I reached up to brush them away when I heard the faint music. It was an old song called "Si tu no estas aqui". I used my jacket sleeve to dry my eyes and peeked out to see Neva already awake, sitting against the wall, listening through her ear buds. "¡Coño! Neva, you woke me up!"

Taking one ear bud out she asked, "What?"

"You woke me up." I slapped the phone off her lap so she'd have to chase it.

"What the *fuck*" She grabbed her phone off the floor and left the room in a huff. I knew she'd forgive me. I tried to go right back to sleep, but it was impossible. I wanted to force my way back into my dream, as if by sheer will. In that moment I wanted to go back so badly, I would have clawed a hole in the universe. It was impossible. I made myself get up, exhausted and absolutely miserable.

Chapter 23

THE ROAD

In the next couple of weeks I finally started
to write the beginnings of a war journal. The war
journals eventually became my books. I also took
up drawing again, something I hadn't done since
high school. These were doodles at first, but then
studies of people around the base, animals,
landscapes, and finally, my own representations.
Once I started I couldn't stop. Watercolor, oil,
colored pencil, just not acrylic. It helped to distract
me, and eventually became a kind of therapy which
continues to this day; art as an act of catharsis.

Miguel gathered us together at this time and
said that Carlos had told him to put together a team
to protect a large cross-country convoy. The
Americans had tried shipping weapons in unmarked
trucks, but there were too many moles in the
military, and the Patriots ended up seizing or
destroying many shipments. As I said elsewhere,
Carlos had become important enough to be involved
in some of the planning activity with the Americans.
I think they trusted his judgment. After the briefest
of explanations, Miguel dismissed everyone else but
asked me to stay, saying, "I want you on this team.
We're headed west, opening up the roads and
resupplying critical facilities. The US Marines want
us in California when we're done. The Americans

have already done a couple of route clearance missions along the way. This is an important operation Alba, and Carlos trusts us to get it done. Also, I think this will be good for us. Our teams could use a little open space." I could only agree. This was an order coming down of course, but I know he wanted to give us some time, and maybe a sense of forward movement again. I thought I might feel more torn, wanting to stay in the fight. The more I thought on it though, the more I welcomed the change of pace.

We received the orders to guard a rotating convoy meant for resupply across the United States, from Virginia straight through to California, using the I-40. The mixed feelings I had at leaving so much undone gave way to the focus of a new mission. We went over the route and regions where we may run into trouble. Although I say this was a convoy, it was staged into many segments, each able to protect itself. Miguel, Neva, Ben, and I were going to be one of the teams protecting the lead portion of the convoy. We would cycle back as each portion of the convoy carrying resupply reached its destination. This would provide protection for different segments, and there were many such groups performing the same activities. As supplies reached their destination, the vehicles providing security would become the largest parts of each segment of the convoy. They would make their way to California to bolster forces in the West.

Miguel, Neva, Ben and a few others would be taking an Einsa Neton 4x4 together. The Neton has no doors, and looks like a VAMTAC and a Jeep had a child. It's very badass. Ours had loitering munitions mounted on the back. There were all manner of vehicles transporting men, equipment, and supplies, with plenty of protection. There were IBERO SMV20s, Pizarros, Dragons, Falcatas, artillery trucks, and more. Drones would provide eyes in the sky. We loaded our gear one clear morning and waited for the first section of the convoy to finish getting ready. The protection vehicles were interspersed throughout the convoy. This included fast reaction vehicles like the Neton and motorbikes. Everyone was spread out to avoid IEDs and ambushes. If anything were to happen, we'd provide covering fire or even assault positions that were close to the road, as long as we did not stray far. The concern when planning this operation had not been random civilians taking shots at us, but coordinated attacks meant to draw us into traps. Such ambushes could be very deadly if well planned. Time was on our side because we were moving fast. That left little time for the enemy to plan. Thus, as we had done throughout the conflict, we talked through every eventuality beforehand. Once we set out to cross the country, however, we needed to stay in motion as much as possible.

Early one morning, after preparing the convoy, we took the I-64 West up to the I-81 South. This was a seemingly endless column of military and support vehicles which must have presented a tempting target for the enemy. There was only one disturbing incident along the I-81, near the tiny city of Buena Vista. A small group opened fire on us from both sides of a bridge as we approached. They were firing from high ground so it was a little difficult to get at them, but they also threw molotov cocktails, and sadly, there were casualties among the British - two injured and two who later died. One Spaniard was also injured. We fired back with airburst grenades, shredding most of them. The incident later took on a sour tone in that region of Virginia because the attackers turned out to be a group of students from a large nearby university. This made us very cautious, resupplying Roanoke with great haste. A number of Canadian and British soldiers parted ways with us there, staying on at small Army and Marine reserve centers in the town, just in case. The plan was to strengthen many of the cities, military bases, and special installations along the way by leaving additional NATO troops and equipment.

Leaving southwestern Virginia, and long into eastern Tennessee, we ended up in several small skirmishes with various militias, but not as serious as the Buena Vista incident. Mostly militiamen would open fire for a moment, then retreat immediately under sustained fire. We never fell for their ambushes, and those who tried to stay and fight, faced harsh consequences. It's all fun and games to fire at a military vehicle with an AR-15, until the return fire from a 40mm chain gun turns you into ground beef. The attacks subsided around the time we reached Dandridge, in eastern Tennessee, where I-81 runs into I-40. Nowhere in Tennessee did we engage any Patriots that I know of, which suggests that they were told not to attack. We resupplied Knoxville quickly in order to also reach "Secret City", the Y-12 National Security Complex in Oak Ridge. Low, green hills met us at the entrance to the complex. The hills ringed a long, shallow, oblong valley, which seemed to have been entirely filled in with buildings and concrete. Y-12 has about 4700 employees and 1500 employees of associated companies – IT, Security, labs, and so on. Months prior, the site had already survived a domestic terrorist attack when a small plane was flown into the warehouse which held highly enriched uranium. Thankfully, their aim was imperfect and the building survived with only minor damage. All the same, we left a small security contingent to bolster their existing forces and delivered plenty of food and other essentials.

We spent the night outside the main area of the Y-12 complex for operational security, then left the next morning. Nashville was the next stop, an attractive city where we left a greater number of soldiers for security. Especially in large cities, those of us who stayed tended to keep out of sight. That way we could alway be deployed as a quick reaction force as needed, without presenting ourselves as a target to the enemy. That evening we parked in a large lot next to a rail yard, where we received additional supplies for the next leg of our trip. The rest of our convoy parked in nearby lots, including the largest one, that had been created for us by moving many of the shipping containers next to the rail yard into protective rings to conceal our vehicles. To prevent tempting an act of terrorism, we removed ourselves from the city in the early morning hours. We pushed on to Memphis, a large city at the western edge of the state, where the Mississippi River divides Tennessee from Arkansas. Just as we had done in Nashville, we left a large group of soldiers and vehicles in Memphis. The next morning our convoy crossed the Hernando de Soto bridge, named after the conquistador who explored the southeast and destroyed a large part of the Mississippian culture by fire, sword, and smallpox in the 1540s. Here we were bringing fire and sword again but this time, I believe, we were on the right side of history. My hope, as always, is that we learn from the past and make wiser choices. The future depends on it.

As we left Memphis we entered Arkansas, which was very green, mostly flat country with many trees. The main objective there was to resupply Little Rock, which was in terrible shape. Militias and the Patriots had attacked the city constantly until it nearly fell to them. There was no opposition until we were about halfway to Little Rock, somewhere in Monroe county I believe. Militias would start small firefights and flee, perhaps hoping to draw us into an ambush. We'd fire back and keep driving. After resupplying Little Rock some vehicles split off from the convoy, taking the I-30 down toward Murfreesboro. There was a park there called Crater of Diamonds.

Apparently the leader of some militia called the Rattlers, named after their football team, had the idea to gather up children and use them as slaves to find diamonds, which were then used like money in the region. The militia used the diamonds to buy weapons and pay mercenaries, while confiscating paper money. At the time I actually wanted to go with the group headed for Murfreesboro, so I could help free those kids. Command gave the orders, however, and I had to follow them. Perhaps I felt like I was on thin ice with leadership, but probably wrongly. Maybe it was some kind of internal tall poppy syndrome. It didn't escape me that I had gained a bit of minor fame by capturing Hahn; noted or notorious, depending on who you'd ask. And anyway, I'm not sure if I would have been happy with the outcome of the Crater of Diamonds operation.

Hearing about the battle around Murfreesboro later, the results were mixed, since some of the kids were used as human shields and foot soldiers by the militia. Many were injured or accidentally killed during the firefights. The Rattlers had already killed so many locals when they arrived, that most of the unaffiliated men were missing, as were attractive women, and anyone storing food and ammo. Every supply that could be taken from the community and hoarded apparently had been. Violence, control of food, and control of information was used to pacify and manipulate the population. As we saw everywhere else, preppers were preyed upon. This is the sadder cousin of the parable of the ant and the grasshopper, where the grasshopper eats all of the ant's food after murdering the colony.

We resupplied Little Rock and tried to talk to local US soldiers to get the lay of the land. Continuing on the I-40, we thought of the militias we heard about in the Ozark National Forest, but we knew it would be better to simply deny them the road than go running into the forest after them. Besides, if we headed north we might only succeed in driving them out of the forest, perhaps toward the Native people and Tulsa. I'm sure none of them wanted a guerrilla war in their town.

Chapter 24

IMPASSE

In Oklahoma there was a feeling in the air of an uncertain menace, like the people there had kept a lot of their powder dry for just such an occasion. The state had exported many fighters to the Patriots, and several important government figures had been run off or killed. A majority of the population seemed ready to fight, but it was unclear what would set them off. Frequent power outages and a drought were not helping the mood I'm sure. Rather than try to immediately pacify the entire state, the powers that be opted to keep things stable, at least for the moment.

We knew we'd need a great deal of outreach to the communities in Oklahoma, and helped our cause greatly by some skilled diplomacy with those we ran across. We had to be content to simply send supplies up to Tulsa and throughout East Oklahoma, including the Muscogee, Cherokee, Choctaw, Chickasaw, Seminole, Osage Reservation, and all the way up to the Quapaw. We also sent a number of soldiers and armor toward Tulsa, which was to help restore order and re-establish authority throughout the city. There had been some racial violence in Tulsa as well as rampant crime, but the Native People had held their own. Overall, I heard from soldiers stationed there, Tulsa was indeed violent but that it became more of a slog of rough quasi-police work over time.

The main convoy entered Oklahoma City to resupply and reinforce Tinker Air Force Base. Without mentioning units or hardware, we had been advised to turn our eye to a possible incursion by Texas. This informed our choice to leave certain units and equipment in place. The resupply of Oklahoma City could proceed from the base, but for added security we dispersed supplies in the city as well, so that everything did not flow from one central location. We encountered no resistance at all, which was strange given the atmosphere.

The next day our convoy left Oklahoma City from Tinker. Off to our right, far in the distance, vast blue clouds dipped low toward the ground. It looked like a storm was coming, and you could feel it in the air. Along the road at several points, we'd see the burnt out wrecks of pickup trucks riddled with bulled holes. A few technical vehicles with Texas flags sat running on the roadside. It was unclear why they were there. The unnerving thing was how the soldiers were sneering at us, leaned up against their trucks, as though they thought they knew something we didn't. We did our best to look back as though we were one long train of grey men. It would do us no good to set off a conflict with Texas there, or conversely to feign weakness and timidity, which invites aggression. So we looked on. In retrospect, I don't think they understood the lopsided capabilities at play.

An announcement came over the radio, Barksdale Air Force Base in Louisiana had been attacked by one of its own returning B-52s. Fifteen B-52s were carpet bombed and destroyed on the ground, sixteen including the traitorous plane which was shot down. Luckily the bulk of the B-52s had been relocated to California, just in case. The Barksdale attack was rumored to be with the blessing and encouragement of Texas. This makes sense, especially when taken together with the near simultaneous and highly suspicious failure of the levee system that nearly destroyed New Orleans. The blame was pinned on the Patriots, but the strategic underpinnings of chaos at the edges of Texas seemed too hard to ignore. In the days following, many refugees from Louisiana tried to make their way into Texas but were refused access. With flooding and rampant disease, turning these people away was sometimes a death sentence. Tens of thousands died in Louisiana and hundreds of thousands were displaced, possibly more than a million.

Once we crossed into Texas, we received a call that Governor Baker's office had contacted our commanders and demanded a meeting. We resupplied Amarillo proper with one small portion of our convoy, while we agreed to meet the Governor at old Amarillo air base, where we could continue resupply as needed. The convoy was ordered to tighten up and increase speed. We arrived before long at the old air field, which had almost entirely been torn down. Other than some low trees, it was all flat, with most buildings gone, but worn old roads remained. The cool morning had passed and it had turned into a hot, hazy day, with the asphalt reflecting the heat back up from the forlorn site. There, not too far from the entrance, were a few black cars surrounded by military vehicles, a large number of State Troopers and Texas National Guard. My eyes went right to their shoulder patch, the dark arrowhead with a capital T. I remembered Fort Barfoot, and my interrogation at the hands of the Patriots, while a man in this uniform had sat in the back. I tabled that thought for the moment, as many questions as it raised. We parked our vehicles in defensive formations since we did not trust the situation. The rest of our convoy was ordered to stay back. I exited the Neton on Miguel's signal. Many others stayed in their vehicles. Our convoy commander, an older man named Obando, went to meet the Governor, so we accompanied at a short distance. They shook hands but the Governor did not welcome us to Texas. In fact, he said that we were invading the United States and, unless we agreed to immediately withdraw all forces, they would arrest us all or take any action necessary.

The Governor had started calm enough, but his speech about invasion got more venomous with each sentence. Our old commander just nodded and tried to defuse the situation. He replied that he didn't want to upset anyone, and that he was told by the US Government to bring supplies to Amarillo.

He invited the Texas National Guard to take some of the supplies for distribution if they did not trust us to deliver them. The Governor began yelling, saying we should keep our treason food, as well as other nonsense.

I remember Miguel tried to interject, saying "We're only here to help", which sent the Governor off on another tirade.

Obando kept listening and asking politely what the Governor would like us to do, since the US President had ordered the mission. He suggested that we would be glad to wait if the Governor and the President could talk the issues out. I just remember wanting to verbally tear into this man, for wearing his ridiculous hat even though he had probably never laid a hand on cattle, for threatening us, and for preventing us from providing aid to his communities. Even his fancy boots were all for show, since I could see no wear on them. He raised his voice to say something about Texas not wanting to start anything but, "We can sure finish it". What hubris this artisanal charro performed! The National Guardsmen tensed up, some gripping their rifles tighter. There were a *lot* more of us. A State Trooper tried to whisper something to the Governor but was ignored. I wanted to say something, to shut down such talk, but it was not my place.

We listened to this absurd back and forth until someone managed to reach a contact in the President's office. After a short call, the Governor bitterly handed back the phone, and told us to leave

Texas immediately. He turned and stalked back to his car, followed by all of the troopers and Texas National Guard getting back into their vehicles. A follow-up call from the President's office, told us to leave Texas immediately as the Governor had asked. The situation was very tense and it was better to let things cool down. We headed back to I-40 and started out for New Mexico. We hadn't gone far when the call went out on every radio, Texas had just seceded.

Considering the timing, this had to have been planned. Governor Baker had released some kind of pre-recorded televised statement to announce the independence of the Republic of Texas, and invited any other states to join him in forming a new union. Apparently there had already been secret negotiations taking place with the southern states, from North Carolina down to Florida. Those states made a weak show of solidarity, with their congressmen and senators announcing they had heard the Texas proposal, but gave no timetable for any decision. In the Governor's announcement, he gave as part of his rationale the idea that the US had been invaded by foreign countries (apparently referring to NATO troops) and that true Patriots needed to rise up to defend America. He intentionally used the word "patriots" as a dog-whistle and a sign of things to come. The Governor also lied and said invading NATO forces were about to use eastern New Mexico as a sort of buffer to preemptively attack

Texas and claimed that it was California who was trying to dominate the country. This is not taking into account that California had not seceded, Texas had no legal right to secede (or occupy other states), and by "California" he meant the USA. The US President was simply operating out of California.

Attempting to drive through the remainder of Texas as fast as we could, we consolidated our massive convoy, tightening up as we left Amarillo behind. Several of our UAVs were called in to escort us the rest of the way. I could see them moving across the now cloudy skies. Even though the drone controllers at the ground station were "in the box" as they say, they were probably almost as tense as if they were with us. Everyone was put on high alert since an attack could come at any time. That's when another warning came through, an announcement that the Texas National Guard was being scrambled, along with local militias, and anyone with a gun and a truck. This was it. We pushed on, past Amarillo. The treeless desolation of the landscape provided little reassurance. I couldn't see anywhere to hide for miles. A call came in that a convoy of military vehicles was assembling and pushing onto I-40. We sped past the tiny settlement of Adrian, until we finally saw two stone pillars with a yellow and red sign over the road: New Mexico.

Chapter 25

HUBRIS

The drought had led to many small towns in eastern New Mexico emptying out, with citizens often moving north to Colorado, or west to Arizona or the coast. The desolation was made more palpable by our race for time: flat, empty land for miles. Once we knew we were being followed, we made contact with the authorities in California who told us to get to Albuquerque as soon as possible. It became clear we wouldn't make it, so a defensive posture was planned. The US President made a call to tell the Texas governor in no uncertain terms that the secession had no legal effect. As I hear it, the call did not go well. Drones spotted a large convoy leaving the Dallas area. There were also reports of fighting at Sheppard Air Force Base, which meant the enemy might receive air cover at any time. We simply wanted to put as many miles as possible between us and Texas before they could catch up to our convoy. Once we passed the tiny town of Santa Rosa I felt a little relief, since the flat, sandy terrain started to rise a little into low rocky hills. This was starting to become better ground for defense. Drones were reportedly headed our way from several locations inside Texas. The Texas convoy was rapidly closing ground on us in two waves. Fast trucks were advancing at double our speed, no doubt filled with gunmen, but we had a head start. A second wave of heavier equipment, such as tanks, APCs, and the like, could try to reach us once the first wave had pinned us down. I'm sure that was their hope. Their great weakness was a lack of perspective. They thought they were just going to fall on our convoy like it was some easy prey to their predator. In fact the reverse was true, and they were advancing on just one part of a highly trained, highly motivated force, better equipped, more experienced, greater in number, and with the full backing of the US military. What were they thinking, that they could keep driving west and sink the Pacific Fleet with small arms fire and gumption? California had already tried to remove anyone suspect, placing them in other regions or letting them go. That's why the President had moved there. That was the whole point.

We were given directions by the Americans, do *not* engage; fire only when fired upon. There was still the possibility they might stop at the border, or turn back, or listen to reason. So we continued on, racing for time. The US Government continued to reach out to the Governor. New Mexico State Police tried to set up spike strips and cruisers to block the I-40 at the Texas border, or at least buy some time. Two road blocks were set up, one not far from the state line, and another just before Tucumcari. Calls for help from the troopers came not long after those forces from Texas came across the New Mexico border. There was nowhere to hide in that country,

217

as it was a vast plain. Militiamen in technical trucks leading the Texan convoy gunned down the police there, cleared their obstacles, and pulled their cruisers off the road. The convoy of Texans had reached hundreds of trucks. Most of these were bristling with armed gunmen. When they reached the more hardened blockade at Tucumcari, the Texans fanned out and engaged in a protracted firefight. Even after defeating all of the State Troopers there, some of the gunmen fired at armed locals, killing dozens.

The radio was very active, so we could hear what was going on as it happened. Aside from those closing on Albuquerque, Texan forces were also branching out from Dallas toward Oklahoma City, Little Rock, and New Orleans. I would have thought that they might press their diplomatic position with their neighbors first, but they opted for force. Perhaps they didn't get the answer they wanted from their neighbors on secession. Perhaps they thought occupation would pressure the Southern states to capitulate and join them. We had left German, French, English, Polish, Spanish, and Italian troops in Oklahoma, at Tinker Air Force Base, to bolster American forces there. They would have to respond to the threat, while we might have to protect Albuquerque. As we sped along, reports came in of attacks on citizens along the I-40 in Newkirk, Cuervo, and Santa Rosa; the Texans were still gaining on us. Finally we pled with the Americans to make a determination on use of force.

Without making a stand and setting an ambush, or at least a line of defense, we would be overrun. Apparently the Americans had hoped to form that line of defense themselves, so they responded that we should join their line east of Albuquerque.

At a bend in the I-40 the terrain became rough rock ledge, and I saw many trees. This place was easier to defend, and I felt a little better about our situation. When a radio call let us know to watch for US Marines ahead, we probably all breathed a little sigh of relief. Somewhere before Tijeras, a US Marine Corp sergeant stood just in front of a road block, flagging us off the main road. He sarcastically said to every vehicle as it passed, "Welcome to Texit".

As we made our way up the path, I saw some Marines in a ULTV who pointed at our Neton and gave a thumbs-up, "Oorah!"

Recognizing a meme-like moment that we couldn't let pass, we pointed back at their ULTV and did the same. The entire convoy continued pulling off the road, miles of vehicles, with many of the supply trucks continuing on to Albuquerque. Flaggers moved each nation's forces into locations which would allow them to fight together with their countrymen. Most of the heavier fighting vehicles were directed to position next to the American formations, as we shuffled assets for advantage over the enemy. NATO forces held the high ground overlooking the I-40. The US Marines told us that their Army and Air Force would also take part in the operation, denying passage from Texas if necessary. There was still the small hope that a fight could be avoided. After our convoy cleared off the road, the Americans placed a large sign a mile out near an unmanned road block that said, "U.S. Army, Restricted Area" and that use of deadly force was authorized. Despite that, we were reminded not to fire.

The weather was hot, with a mix of clouds leaving small shadows on the ground, some of which I mistook for vehicles headed up the road. I watched the horizon for a long time with a good pair of binoculars. Seeing nothing, I handed them off to Rafael. Spotting something in the sky, he handed them back so I could take a look. We saw two faint dots, MQ-9 Reaper drones coming from the East, but we were told to stand down. They were sent by Texas, but they had been built and programmed in California. No one mentioned what was happening in the moment, but it turned out their systems had been hacked by US forces with the help of the manufacturer, and they flew over us harmlessly. Only then, some called out what had occurred, and then we knew. Everyone who had crouched down as they passed, stood up and cheered as they continued on without incident, headed west.

I talked to Rafael for a while, and we ate an MRE to pass the time and subdue any anxiety. Miguel and Neva were not far from us, and we all did our best to get ready. After a very long wait, we were told the enemy convoy was approaching. A wind had caked fine dust on my face by that point. At first we saw nothing, even using binoculars. Eventually, like a heat mirage, a faint dust cloud rose on the horizon, slowly followed by the glint of windshields. The Texas convoy was approaching. They had been told, by their own governor, that we were an invading army and we needed to be stopped. It was no wonder they believed this lie but they had been lied to before, I knew it. Big lies don't arrive all at once, they build. All of the ignorance had flowed into this one moment: tiny drops of falsehood becoming rivulets of false conclusions, streams of false stories becoming rivers of misunderstanding.

They must not have been raised to seek out truth because otherwise they may have seen that we were called to this country to help. In lieu of truth, they must have followed the kinds of stories, traditions, and rumors that lead one astray. Traditions and stories *can* help people navigate the world if they hold some deeper truth. Unfortunately, when a story doesn't have the right conclusion you won't know it, because the story will never tell you that part. It is the same with traditions. Falsehoods be damned; if you don't know, say nothing.

Someone yelled out, pointing upward to the Western sky. I looked over to see four faint V-shaped formations following one after another, headed by a B-1 and three B-52s, with each bomber flanked by F-35s and F-22s. My eyes drifted back down to the convoy, still quite small in the distance. Perhaps it was because I had those moments to reflect, but instead of the righteousness I felt when we faced the Patriots at Fort Barfoot, I felt a faint tug of empathy. Those bomber formations were true - mathematically true. There was nothing false about the consequences coming, and no argument would sway the formations from their path. Yes, the Texans had lied to themselves, but they were also lied to. They were lied to because it was useful to someone else, and this made me ambivalent. Anyway, it was too late for them to turn back. Killing the New Mexico troopers, as well as the civilians, had sealed their fate. Their river of falsehoods would end there, poured out uselessly into the desert.

Chapter 26

PACIFIC

The convoy had gotten close enough to see the drivers through the binoculars when the bombers passed us. It was already over for the Texans, even though they continued on. I'll never know if any of them saw the bombers in advance. I only know they kept driving. We all sank as close to the ground as we could, crouching or laying flat, until rocks bit into our flesh. I stayed down but kept watching through the binoculars until small bombs silently fell from each bay. Wave upon wave of bombs filled the air in slanted columns, silhouetted against the sky, drifting in unison toward the ground like rain. As they neared the ground the trucks swerved, cutting left and right, trying to avoid their fate. Some of the gunmen even jumped from their vehicles and sprinted away from the road, trying to reach the rocky ledges where they hoped for shelter. I could see some of the Texan's faces, looking up, then down at the terrain as they ran, then up again. One man's face I'll never forget, young, stubbly beard, terrified eyes, mouth agape, gripping his rifle in one hand as he tried to drop to the ground. There was no escape, and the end came swiftly. Deafening explosions started to envelope the convoy, orange fireballs immediately swallowed by brown and gray clouds, sending endless shock waves straight through us. The entire line of vehicles was swallowed whole. Fire sprung from each truck, and the gray smoke was overtaken by jet black. As the convoy burned furiously I couldn't see a single person moving. Everyone cheered, loudly claiming both victory, and the simple fact that they were still alive.

We drove down to the site in case anyone had survived. We'd need to administer medical treatment or detain anyone who didn't shoot at us. The heat was intense with fires still burning, and the acrid smoke was overwhelming. Approaching the front of the wreckage there was not one single person who remained alive, only the vehicles and corpses remained. The Americans did capture many in the very rear of the Texan column who had been straggling behind. Some of the US soldiers were killed by Texans who had scrambled into well concealed positions, sniping as many as they could before being killed or captured. All I saw among the jumbled remains of the convoy were corpses burning, not a common site even in war. Their expressions were twisted by shock and excruciating pain, some men's blackened fingers still clenching weapons as they crumbled away, while the fires blazed on. We received orders to immediately reform our convoy and continue on to Albuquerque, since there was nothing more we could do there. None of us had much to say as we got back in formation and prepared to leave.

We got into Albuquerque at night, meeting up with a Mr. Hernandez there, who served as mayor. He was quite good natured, probably enjoying the kind of relief felt only by those who escape the fate he and his city had almost suffered. Since New Mexico already had plenty of food supplied by California we stationed a significant number of troops and equipment in the city, with enough firepower to defend against any more Texan incursions. Some of them were posted at Sandia National Laboratory in Albuquerque, while others headed North, past Santa Fe, toward Los Alamos National Laboratory.

As an immediate and temporary blockade against Texas, some American got the idea to use a large gate of trees, felled and chained together, on the I-40 to prevent any Texas forces from reaching Albuquerque. These kinds of blockades are called an abatis, and one was thrown together between the rocky hills just before a curve in the I-40 near a place called Carlito Springs. This was very near our battle against Texas. A passthrough was made of course, to allow vehicles through, but it could be closed to prevent armored vehicles from easily proceeding. The Great Abatis, or "the Gate" as they sometimes called it, was constructed behind our battlefield by using bulldozers to rearrange the terrain and from trees cut out of the Cibola National Forest. For a short time, a strong military presence defended the entire area against Eastern incursions, with the checkpoint able to rain down lethal force, ringed by an outer perimeter of checkpoints with long range non-lethal technology like blinding lasers and LRAD. I know that it was partially dismantled soon after, but while it lasted it was a thing to behold. I never saw it myself, since it was built after we pressed on, but I've seen the pictures. Another spectacle that has been cleaned up in the years since (which can be seen in some of the original photos) are the destroyed enemy vehicles pulled off the highway, no doubt by crane, onto the hills just before reaching the Great Abatis. These jumbled wrecks were laid out thickly and haphazardly along the nearby ledges and mountains, no doubt to have a deterrent effect. Travelers along that stretch today will see no such thing, except just after sunrise when little bits of metal and plastic left behind on the mountains glow orange in the morning light.

Starting out before dawn the next day, we crossed into the rocky desert of Arizona. Short trees, and even grass, began to line the roadside as we neared Flagstaff. A small contingent of our own troops were stationed in the city and we all spent the night there uneventfully. US soldiers were numerous in Arizona, and it felt relatively safe. The next day, those of us not staying left early for California. The remainder of our drive away from Flagstaff was calm, and I was surprised to see the land was covered thickly by pines. Eventually this gave way to flat desert and back to rocky hills again. We listened to music, snacked, and talked to pass the time, but nothing else of importance happened until we got to a low bridge across the Colorado River. Miguel told us this was Arizona's borderline, so we had finally made it.

Entering California, the desert was like a furnace. It passed by us endlessly until we went through the small city of Barstow, before finally joining Route 15. A contingent of our convoy split off and headed north toward Lawrence Livermore National Laboratories in Livermore, California. My mood, which had been blank, improved as the main convoy continued down through Victorville and finally Hesperia. Distant mountains, baking in the afternoon sunlight, closed in on every side as we drove. Around the bend of a mountain pass, the landscape ahead finally started to turn green again as we took Route 215. That was the first point I started to feel truly safe and my vigilance subsided.

Making our way down into the green valley, we passed through the city of San Bernardino. This was closer to what I thought California would be like. Green vines draped the concrete walls of the freeway, decked in red, orange, and pink flowers, whose colors were so shocking in the pastel sunlight that they seemed unreal. The traffic was a bit rough, but we faced no threats there. LA was not what I thought either. Just as a hydra has many heads, Los Angeles is a city of cities. Rather than a coherent whole, it is like a great low-slung beast whose dense buildings passed endlessly by like scales, with occasional spikes of skyscrapers rising from its back. This beast basks under the desert sun at the feet of magnificent mountains, protecting its jewel, the Pacific ocean.

We pulled into Camp Pendleton in the afternoon. It all felt so different from the adrenaline of battle, or the grinding purgatory of waiting. Even on base, the slower pace of commerce and entertainment could be seen everywhere. We all noted that civilization goes on, despite the soldiers coming and going. The US Marines gave us cards for the MCX, and showed us to our quarters. We went clothes shopping, which was surreal. I felt like I needed to walk through each aisle and carefully figure out how to dress myself again. What did I want to wear? In the end I shrugged and gave up, picking out a pair of jeans and a green t-shirt. At least they fit me well. Miguel got Neva and I to go with him to buy an iPhone. While we were there I paid to have Neva's screen fixed, having cracked it before our journey from the East Coast.

Over a loud dinner at a barbecue restaurant, a group of us made plans to go to Malibu the next day. It was surreal to experience this place of such calming peace, and the slow pace of real life, so shortly after facing death. We were told to get some rest that night but we knew that the beach was nearby. Our group, all FGNE, decided to go down to the water at sunset. There was no way to keep us from reaching the ocean that evening.

Arriving at the beach, we kicked off our boots and socks to walk in the sand, enjoying that feeling on our bare feet. Miguel shot us a look, paused a moment, then pulled out his phone. After a little scrolling, he looked back up. He started to play the Spanish National Anthem, and I got it. It happened to be the Franco era version with lyrics, but it took on an altered meaning that night. I think Miguel started, but when we heard "¡Viva España!" we all joined in without shame, singing the words proudly. A few civilians looked on from a distance. Their heads tilted and their posture changed as they heard us sing, perhaps understanding the words and maybe even the meaning. I thought about all those soldiers, from many nations, who had worked so hard and made such sacrifices as they crossed America, trying to maintain civilization. I thought, how far we had come across forest and mountain and desert! Perhaps that's why the final line of our anthem, which we sang with the most feeling, struck me: "Glory to the fatherland that knew how to follow, over the blue sea, the path of the sun!" We felt that this was the very moment we were living through. Those of us who made it.

The sunset was bold, red and yellow melting into the ocean. My mind drifted to the unfinished inscription on my knife, "*Alba ,* ". The mask started to slip and I felt myself missing Hugo; it was a raw feeling, overwhelming. Looking out across the water I was finally still. A sense of ease washed over me. I let go of everything - the anger, the guilt, and the wall. My smile had faded. I slowly made my way down the beach toward the water. Walking out into the ocean, the cold of the clear water shocked me, but I kept going as if in a trance. The others called out my name at first, but began to follow me in quietly. There was no running or laughing, just the calm. I still felt the waves pushing against me, till I was nearly waist deep. As I edged a little further out I began to cry, softly at first, then bitterly. I felt Neva's hand slip onto my shoulder, then others. I could finally admit to myself all that I had wanted. Too late. We all felt the weight of that moment as it happened and I could hear some of the others crying too, for reasons both shared and deeply personal. Our sighs merged with the evening air, and our tears were lost in the sea. Over that we heard the constant washing of waves, mirroring the sound of palms above rustling in the warm breeze. The sky was mixing into beautiful greens and blues, as the shadows of calling sea-birds wheeled dimly against the clouds. Beyond the twilight, stars began to glitter above us in the darkening sky.

Our arrival in California occurred on the 20th of September, of the third year of the Second American Civil War.